THE ORCHARD BOOK OF FAIRY TALES

In the same series

THE ORCHARD BOOK OF NURSERY RHYMES
Compiled by Zena Sutherland   Illustrated by Faith Jaques

THE ORCHARD BOOK OF GREEK MYTHS
Geraldine McCaughrean   Illustrated by Emma Chichester Clark

THE ORCHARD BOOK OF NURSERY STORIES
Sophie Windham

THE ORCHARD BOOK OF FAIRY TALES

Retold by
ROSE IMPEY

Illustrated by
IAN BECK

ORCHARD BOOKS

For Sue Flahey and Michaela Morgan
– for their help and support –
and for Katie White's class,
Birstall Highcliffe School,
a critical audience

R.I.

For Jean, in remembrance

I.B.

ORCHARD BOOKS
338 Euston Road, London NW1 3BH
Orchard Books Australia
Hachette Children's Books
Level 17/207 Kent Street, Sydney, NSW 2000
First published in Great Britain in 1992
First paperback publication in 1994
This edition first published in 2005
ISBN 1 84362 181 9
Text © Rose Impey 1992
Illustrations © Ian Beck 1992, 2005
The right of Rose Impey to be identified as the author and of Ian Beck to be identified as the illustrator
of this work has been asserted by them in accordance with the Copyright, Designs and Patents Act, 1988.
A CIP catalogue record for this book is available from the British Library.
10 9 8 7 6 5 4 3 2
Printed in Malaysia

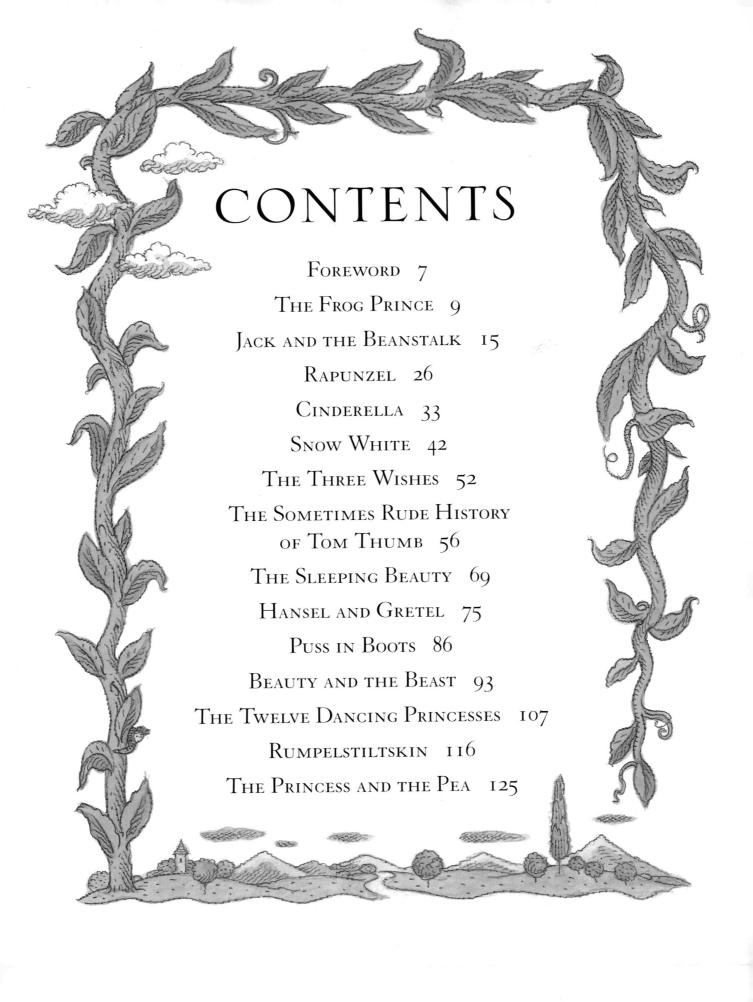

CONTENTS

Foreword 7

The Frog Prince 9

Jack and the Beanstalk 15

Rapunzel 26

Cinderella 33

Snow White 42

The Three Wishes 52

The Sometimes Rude History
of Tom Thumb 56

The Sleeping Beauty 69

Hansel and Gretel 75

Puss in Boots 86

Beauty and the Beast 93

The Twelve Dancing Princesses 107

Rumpelstiltskin 116

The Princess and the Pea 125

SOURCES FOR THE TALES

"The Frog Prince", "Rapunzel", "Snow White", "The Sleeping Beauty",
"Hansel and Gretel", "The Twelve Dancing Princesses" and
"Rumpelstiltskin"
Kinder- und Haus-Marchen
Jacob Grimm (1785–1863) and Wilhelm Grimm (1786–1859)

"Jack and the Beanstalk"
English Fairy Tales Joseph Jacobs (1854–1916)

"Cinderella" and "Puss in Boots"
Histoires ou Contes du temps passé Charles Perrault (1628–1703)

"The Three Wishes" and "Beauty and the Beast"
Magasin des enfants Madame Leprince de Beaumont (1711–1780)

"The Sometimes Rude History of Tom Thumb"
Richard Johnson's version reproduced in the Opies' *Classic Fairy Tales*

"The Princess and the Pea"
Tales Told for Children Hans Andersen (1805–1875)

FOREWORD

Some of the stories in this collection are among the oldest in the world—the Cinderella story, in a Chinese version, dates back as early as 850 A.D. It might seem extraordinary that such old stories, divorced as they are from the material details of life today, should have any real relevance for modern children. But fairy tales continue to speak to new generations because they contain important universal truths which help those who hear them to make sense of their own lives and inner feelings, and do it in a way that young children can understand.

When these tales were first told they were passed by word of mouth from one generation to another and from community to community. At each telling they were adapted to the audience and when they came to be written down they were again reshaped, and often refined, by literary scholars like Charles Perrault and the Brothers Grimm, who made their own distinctive mark on them, to such an extent that these versions have come to be seen as the "correct" or "proper" ones. But it is in the nature of these stories that they have resisted being pinned down too precisely. Wherever they are retold to a new audience, when told with affection and integrity, the stories have a new life.

This collection includes the most popular and well-known of the fairy tales, ranging from the romance and elegance of "Beauty and the Beast" to the knockabout humour of "The Three Wishes" and the epic adventure of "Tom Thumb". Each of the stories, because they are all so different, requires its own voice.

It has been a wonderful experience, to work on what are arguably some of the best tales ever told. As a storyteller, I responded directly to the stories themselves, choosing to work from whichever source spoke most effectively to me. Over the years many other writers have reworked these stories for a new audience. This collection is part of that ongoing process.

Rose Impey

THE FROG PRINCE

In the olden days, when wishing still did some good, there was a king and he had a string of daughters. They were all beautiful, but the youngest was the most beautiful. Even the sun, which had seen some things in its time, blinked whenever it shone into her lovely face.

When the weather was hot and this youngest princess wanted to be cool, she used to wander into a nearby wood and sit in the shade of a tree, by the edge of a deep well. Now, it happened one day that she was sitting there, playing with a golden ball—throwing it up and catching it, throwing it up and catching it—when it slipped through her fingers, fell into the well and completely disappeared.

This ball was the most treasured thing she had in the world. The girl was so distraught she began to sob as if her heart would break.

Suddenly, up popped a great ugly frog.

"What's wrong, my beauty?" asked the frog. "That crying's enough to melt the heart of a stone."

"I've lost my ball. It's fallen into the well and it's so deep I can't even see the bottom. I'll never get it back."

"I can get it back," said the frog. "It's easy."

The princess stopped crying.

Then the frog said, "But what will you give me if I do?"

"My clothes, my pearls and jewels, even this golden crown on my head, anything."

"Anything?" asked the frog.

"Anything in the world," said the princess.

"Jewels and golden crowns are no use to me," said the frog. "But if you promise to be my wife . . ."

"Your wife!" The princess nearly burst out laughing.

"If you let me live with you and eat off your little golden plate and drink from your little golden cup, and sleep in your own little bed . . . then I'll get it back for you."

The princess thought he must be joking. Marry a frog! It was too silly. Anyway, how could a frog live away from its well? But then she thought, 'Why not humour him?' She would promise him anything, if he would only get her ball.

"Yes, yes," she said, "whatever you like."

The frog closed his big goggle eyes and dived deep into the well. And, in less than the time it takes to tell, he reappeared with the ball in his wide-open mouth. But when he threw the ball down, the princess snatched it up and ran off home with it.

"Wait, wait," called the frog. "I can't run as fast as you."

And that was exactly what the princess was relying on. She was soon safe at home and never gave the frog another thought.

But, as you well know, we can't wriggle out of our promises that easily; and neither could she.

The next evening, as the princess sat down for dinner with her family, she heard a flip, flap, flop, coming up the steep marble staircase, then a gentle tapping low down at the door.

There came a croaking voice, which the princess recognised, and it said, "Open the door, youngest born."

The princess ran to the door and opened it. But when she saw the frog sitting there, she slammed the door shut and hurried back to her place at the table. She sat there shaking, as if she'd seen her own ghost.

"My dear," said the king. "Who was it? You look as if an ogre had come to carry you away."

"Almost as bad, father," said she. "It's a great ugly frog that I met yesterday. I lost my golden ball in the well and, because I was so upset, he got it back for me. But, in return, he made me promise to marry him and let him live with me."

Just then the voice came again:

"Open the door, my love, my life.
Open the door, sweet lady.
Remember you swore to be my wife.
That was the promise you made me."

"Well," said the king. "A promise is a promise and must be kept. Let the frog in."

The princess went and opened the door and in hopped the frog, flip, flop, flip, flop, across to the table. Then it said,

"Lift me up, my love, my life.
Lift me up, sweet lady.
I want to sit in the lap of my wife.
Remember the promise you made me."

But the princess couldn't even bring herself to touch the clammy frog and she went on sitting there, ignoring him, until the king insisted.

"A promise is a promise and must be kept."

So she took the frog up on her knee. But next he wanted to be on the table, and then, when he was on the table, he still wasn't satisfied.

"Move your plate closer, my love, my life,
Share your food with me, sweet lady.
Such is the act of a loving wife.
Remember the promise you made me."

The princess knew she would have to do it, yet she hated every moment. She sat there, hardly able to look at him. The frog ate a hearty meal, but the food stuck in the princess's throat, so that she felt she would be sick.

When the great ugly frog had eaten until he was quite bloated with food, he said:

"Take me to bed, my love, my life.
Take me to bed, sweet lady.
From now on you are my wife.
Remember the promise you made me."

At this the princess began to cry. The thought of that cold, wet creature in her own little bed was too much to bear. She couldn't do it; she wouldn't do it; no one could make her. But the king could. He was angry.

"This is no way to treat someone who helps you when you most need it. Don't look down on him now."

So the princess picked up the frog between two fingers and held him at a distance. This way she carried him all the way up the stairs until they were alone in her bedroom. Then she placed the frog in the corner, farthest from her bed, and hoped he would stay there.

But later, when she was lying in the dark, the frog crept over, flip, flop, flip, flop, and said, "Princess, lift me up and let me sleep with you in your little bed. I'll be more comfortable there." The princess hesitated, but the frog added, "Or I'll tell your father."

And the princess knew only too well what the king would say. So she lifted the frog up and placed him beside her on the pillow. Then she squeezed herself on to the very edge of the bed, as far as she could from the clammy creature.

But now, horror of horrors, what do you think he said next?

"Come much closer, my love, my life,
Come much closer, sweet lady.
Kiss my lips, my own dear wife.
Remember the promise you made me."

At this the princess was in an agony of disgust. But she closed her eyes and turned her face to the detested animal. Determined to get it over as quickly as she could, she pursed up her lips ready and leaned forward.

For a moment she allowed herself to imagine the feel of his cold, wet skin against her own. It made her shiver. But when her lips touched his she was amazed to feel instead that they were soft and warm, certainly not frog-like.

The princess opened her eyes. She expected to be looking into the great goggle eyes of the frog, but she wasn't. She was looking into the dark, smiling eyes of a handsome prince. Oh, the relief!

Then he told her such a story, of how he had been enchanted by a wicked fairy and destined to stay that way until a princess rescued him. And she'd been the one to do it.

Well, with her so beautiful and him so handsome, you'll soon guess the outcome. He asked her to marry him and return with him to his father's kingdom. And the next day there arrived the most elegant coach with eight plumed horses to pull it, which carried them home. There they lived happily for the rest of their lives. And if they lived happily, well then, why shouldn't we also?

JACK AND THE BEANSTALK

There was once a poor widow who had nothing in the world but a son called Jack and a cow called Milky-White. Jack was no help. He was a dreamer; he couldn't keep a job for two days together. But Milky-White was a good milking cow and saved them both from starving. However, the time came when the cow grew too old and her milk dried up. Then there was trouble.

"Now we're ruined," said the poor widow.

"I'll get a job, mother," said Jack.

"We've tried *that* before," said his mother. "No, there's nothing left but to sell the cow."

"Leave it to me," said Jack. "I'm just the lad to strike a bargain." And the same day he set off for market.

Well, Jack hadn't gone very far when he met a little old man, and couldn't he talk!

"Good morning, good morning and what a morning for a bargain. You look a smart lad," said he. "Where are you going with that fine cow?"

"To market," said Jack.

"I might be able to save you the trip," said the man.

This news pleased Jack; he was already feeling weary.

"And because I like the look of you and that *handsome* cow," said the little old man, "I'm going to give you such a bargain. What do

you think of these?" And he held out his fist, opened his fingers, and there in his palm were five . . . beans.

"Beans?" said Jack.

"Beans!" said the man. "Not just one bean, not two beans, not even three nor four," said the man, "but five beans is the bargain and you won't get a better one."

"Five beans for my cow? You must think I'm daft," said Jack.

"These aren't any old beans," said the fast-talking man. "Believe me, these are magic beans. Plant them overnight and by morning they'll have grown into a beanstalk that'll make a hole in the sky."

Well, the word magic caught Jack's imagination. He took a closer look at the beans. They shimmered like a rainbow. They looked magic, all right.

"It's a deal," he said, and he pocketed the beans, handed over the cow and was home before his mother had finished her work.

"Back already?" she said, amazed. "I hope you got a good price."

"You'll never believe it, mother," said Jack, bursting with excitement.

"Oh, Jack," said she with relief. "How much did you get? Ten pounds? Fifteen? Surely not twenty?"

"Better than that, mother," said he. And he opened his hand with a flourish and showed her the five beans. His mother was speechless. But not for long.

"Beans!" she yelled. "Beans? You sold my pride and joy for a handful of beans? You idiot. You fool. You nincompoop!"

Jack's mother snatched the beans out of Jack's hand and threw them through the open door.

"That's what I think of your precious beans. Up to bed with you. There'll be no supper tonight. Or any other night from now on." And she sat in the kitchen and wept with temper and hunger combined.

Jack climbed the stairs, a sad and hungry boy, but more sorry for his mother than his own empty stomach.

Next morning when Jack woke he wondered where on earth he was. The little window which usually let in the morning sun cast a green glow over the room, as if it were under the sea. Jack slipped out of bed and across to the window. Outside an enormous beanstalk twisted and twined its way into the sky, breaking through the clouds, its stalk as thick as the trunk of a full-grown tree.

Clearly, Jack had been right to trust the beans, and he didn't hesitate now. He reached out into the branches, pulled himself up and disappeared among the dense leaves.

Jack climbed and he climbed and he climbed for most of the day until, utterly exhausted, he reached the top of the beanstalk. There

was nothing in sight but a wide, winding road. Jack walked along the road until at last he came to a huge great house, and at the door of the huge great house was a huge great woman.

"Good morning," said Jack, nice and polite. "I'm almost dead from hunger. Please, could you give me a mouthful of something?"

"It's a mouthful you want, is it? It's a mouthful you'll *be* if my husband catches you," said the huge great woman. "He's an ogre. He eats boys like you on toast."

"I'll just have to take my chance," said Jack. "I'm dead anyway if I don't have something to eat. You wouldn't want that on your conscience, would you?" And Jack gave her the kind of smile that would charm any ogre's wife.

"Oh, all right," said she. "But be sharp. He could be back any time."

She led Jack into the kitchen and gave him a bowl of porridge. But as soon as he started to eat, the bowl, the table, the whole kitchen began to shake.

"Quick, here he comes now. Into the oven with you. And not a sound or it'll be toasted boy sandwich and no mistake."

Before he could object, the ogre's wife had bundled Jack into the oven, leaving the door open the tiniest crack.

The shuddering came closer and closer.

Thump! Thump! Thump! Thump!

Jack heard a voice like thunder booming down a tunnel:

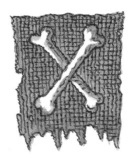

"Fee-fi-fo-fum,
I smell the blood of an Englishman.
Be he alive, or be he dead,
I'll grind his bones to make my bread."

The ogre thumped the table. "Where is he, wife?"

"There's no one here," said she. "That's leftovers you can smell—last night's stew. Come and eat your breakfast."

Then she set in front of him a dozen chickens piled high on a dish. The hungry ogre ate, smacking his lips and snapping and crunching the bones until Jack thought he would faint from the noise.

After he had eaten, the ogre took out a bag of gold, emptied it on to the table and counted it over and over again. Jack peeped through the crack and watched the ogre. But mostly he watched the shining gold, and thought of all the things he and his mother could buy with it.

At last the ogre laid his head on the table and fell asleep, his snores rumbling round the room.

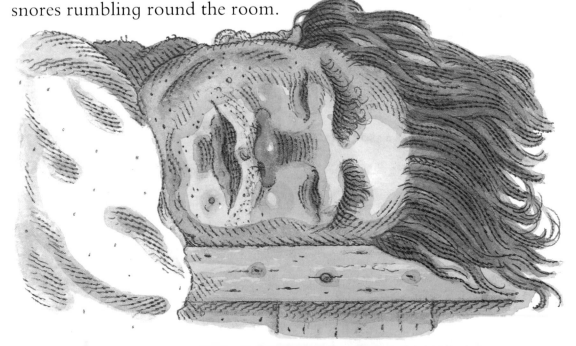

Then Jack lost no time in escaping. He slipped out of the oven, swung the sack of gold over his shoulder and set off for home. He ran as fast as he could, despite the great weight, until he reached the top of the beanstalk. Jack lowered himself into its branches and began to climb down.

When Jack's mother saw him safe and sound she hugged him and kissed him. Then, when she thought of the worry he'd caused her, she scolded him and smacked him. But when she saw the sack of gold she hugged and kissed him even harder.

"Oh, Jack," said she.

"Oh, mother," said he, "give up." Jack wasn't one for kissing and cuddling. Still, he was glad to see his mother happy.

For quite a long while Jack and his mother lived well on the gold, but in time it was gone. Isn't that always the way with money?

So now they were poor again, and Jack wanted to go back up the beanstalk. His mother wouldn't hear of it, of course; but that didn't stop Jack.

One day, without a word, off he went, climbing his weary way to the top. He'd forgotten what a way it was, and when he reached the huge great house he was almost too tired to speak.

The same as last time, standing at the door, was the ogre's wife.

"Good morning," said Jack.

The huge great woman, being shortsighted, bent down and peered at Jack. "There was a young lad," said she, "looked remarkably like you, came here once before and stole my husband's gold."

"What a scoundrel," said Jack, looking as if butter wouldn't melt in his mouth. "I bet I know that lad. If you'd give me a bite to eat I could tell you a thing or two about him."

Well, the ogre's wife didn't know whether to believe Jack or not. But he had such a way with him that once more she found herself taking him in and giving him a bowl of porridge to eat.

Just as before, there came a shuddering and a juddering. All the plates rattled on the shelves.

"Quick," said the ogre's wife. And she bundled him into the oven again.

Not a moment too soon. In came the ogre. This time you should have heard him sniff!

"Fee-fi-fo-fum," said he. "I can smell him, wife, I can smell him."

"Surely it's only those lads you had last week and enjoyed so much. How the smell of boys does linger round the place," said his wife. "Sit down, your breakfast's ready for you."

So the ogre, still sniffing and snuffing, sat at the table and ate a pair of sheep.

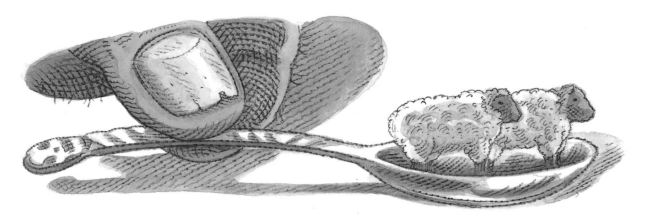

When he was done he called to his wife, "Bring me the hen that lays the golden eggs."

As soon as it was on the table the ogre said, "Lay." And the hen laid a perfect golden egg. Again he said, "Lay." And it laid another, and another, each time he spoke, until there was quite a pile of them. Tiring of this, the ogre fell asleep with his head on the table, his snores like a gale howling through the house.

Jack had again watched everything through the crack in the oven door. Now he crept out, tucked the hen under his arm, and set off at a run. He headed for the beanstalk and home before the ogre could wake and catch him.

This time Jack found his mother nearly frantic with worry. But he hugged her and kissed her and promised her anything if only she wouldn't be cross with him.

"Wait till you see this, mother," said he. "Stand there, don't move, just watch. Now, hen," he said, "lay."

And the hen laid a perfect golden egg. And another and another, and she went on laying until the house was ankle deep in them.

Well, as you'll realise, this time the money didn't run out because if it did Jack had only to say, "Lay," and there would always be more. But the truth is Jack had a longing to go back up the beanstalk, and nothing his poor mother said could persuade him out of it.

One morning, while she was still asleep, Jack set off again. When he reached the huge great house he knew better than to try his luck a third time. Instead he waited in the garden until the ogre's wife came out of the house. Then he slipped in behind her back and hid, not in the oven, but in a large cooking pot on top of the stove.

It wasn't long before the ogre and his wife came into the kitchen.

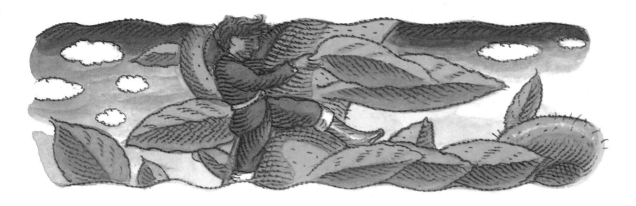

Thump! Thump! Thump! Thump!

  "Fee-fi-fo-fum,
  I smell the blood of an Englishman."

"I smell him, wife, this time I *know* I smell him."

"Well, dear, if it's that rascal who stole your gold and the hen that lays the golden eggs, he's sure to be in the oven."

But when they looked in the oven, Jack wasn't there, nor anywhere else in the kitchen they thought to look. At last his wife persuaded the ogre to have his meal and forget about boys.

The ogre reluctantly sat down, but he couldn't settle. Several times he got up and searched again. One time he even had his hand on the lid of the cooking pot. Jack stopped breathing and imagined himself sandwiched between two slices of toast.

But just then the ogre's wife came in. "Sit yourself down and tuck into this," said she. "This'll take your mind off troublesome boys."

She set in front of him half a horse. The ogre sat down, but still he muttered, "I could have sworn I smelled a boy."

When he had eaten, the ogre's wife brought him his magic harp.

"This is what you need," said she. "This'll calm you down."

No sooner was it on the table than the harp began to play all on its own. It played the most soothing and beautiful music Jack had ever heard. In no time, the ogre was lulled into such a deep sleep that his snores caused only the lightest breeze.

Jack carefully climbed out of the cooking pot and tiptoed over to the table. He was determined to have the harp for himself and his mother. But the moment he touched it the harp called out, "Master! Master!"

Jack didn't stop. He grabbed the harp and ran, as fast as he could, back towards the beanstalk. The ogre was soon behind him. Still dozy from sleep, he stumbled several times and nearly fell so that Jack reached the beanstalk and was climbing down before the ogre arrived at the top.

For a second the ogre hesitated. Trust his great weight to a beanstalk, he thought, not likely! But again the harp cried out, "Master! Master!"

Then the ogre began to follow Jack, swinging down the beanstalk so that it swayed from side to side.

When Jack dared to look up, he saw two huge great boots breaking through the clouds. That made him move even faster. As he slithered down towards the lowest branches he shouted, "Mother! Mother! Bring me an axe."

Jack's mother rushed out of the cottage carrying the axe. When *she* looked up and saw the ogre's huge great legs coming through the clouds, she almost fainted. But Jack was down by now and seized the axe from her.

He chopped once, twice, clean through the beanstalk. For a moment it seemed to hang in the sky, then it crashed to the ground, bringing the ogre with it. He fell head first with such force that he was buried to the waist, legs in the air—stone dead. And that was the end of him.

So, with more money than they could ever spend and the harp to keep them always happy, Jack and his mother had nothing left to wish for, except for Jack to marry, which in time he did. And then, since three can live as well as two, they all lived together and may still be doing so, for all I know.

RAPUNZEL

It is a hard thing to want a child and never to have one. There was once a couple who had all but given up hope when at last the wife became pregnant and it seemed as if their prayers had been answered.

As the months passed, the woman spent many hours sitting at her bedroom window, which overlooked a neighbouring garden. It was full of fine vegetables and beautiful flowers, but it was entirely surrounded by a high wall to keep out trespassers. The garden belonged to a powerful witch, and everyone was afraid of her.

One summer's day, as the woman looked down on the lush green vegetables, her gaze fell on a bed of delicious rapunzel plants. They looked so tempting that the woman couldn't take her eyes off them. Oh, what she would give for a taste of them!

Soon she had a craving for the plant, which is sometimes the way with pregnant women. She wouldn't eat anything else. She began to look pale and weak.

"What's wrong, my dear?" asked her husband, who hated to see her unhappy.

"I must have some of that rapunzel," she told him, "otherwise I think I might die."

Now the man was in a dilemma. He couldn't see his wife waste away for the sake of a few rapunzel plants. But the thought of stealing into that forbidden garden chilled his heart. At last, however, it was clear he had no choice.

Late one night the man climbed the high wall and dropped silently to the ground. He crept through the vegetable plot and snatched a handful of the plants, then stole away with them, his heart beating fast.

When she saw the rapunzel his wife fell upon it and ate it as if she hadn't eaten for a week, which was almost the case.

But even then she wasn't satisfied. She must have more. Nothing else would do.

So the next night the poor man had to go again. Imagine his horror this time when he dropped cat-like from the wall to find the witch there, waiting for him.

"Now I've caught you," she said. "Steal from me, would you? You'll live to regret this."

"Spare me, please have mercy. I'm not really a thief. I only came out of desperation, to save my wife, who is pregnant. Without your rapunzel plants I thought she would die."

When the witch heard this she changed her tune entirely.

"Why, help yourself. Take as much as you want. Come as often as you like."

For a moment the man looked relieved, until he heard what else she had to say.

"But in exchange you must give me the baby when it is born." Then the man looked distraught. What kind of exchange was that?

"Don't worry," said the witch, "I'll love the child and care for it like a mother. Come now, what do you say?"

What could he say? The poor man was terrified of the witch, and before he knew what had happened he had promised the baby to her. Then there was no going back.

When it was time, the woman gave birth to a little girl, and soon the witch came to claim her. No amount of pleading could persuade the witch to leave the child. The couple had made their bargain; now they must stick to it. The witch named her Rapunzel, after the plants that had caused all the trouble, and took the child away to live with her.

The girl grew very beautiful, strong and healthy, with long hair the colour of molten gold that fell like a river way past her waist. The witch kept her word; she did care for the girl, and loved her like a mother.

When Rapunzel reached twelve she was so beautiful that the witch couldn't bear to share her with anyone. She took the girl to live in a high tower in the middle of a wood. It had neither a door nor a staircase, only a window at the very top, so that no one else could ever reach her.

Each day, when the witch visited, she would stand below the girl's window and call out:

"Rapunzel, Rapunzel, let down your hair."

Then the girl, whose hair was longer than ever, wrapped it twice around a window hook and lowered it more than twenty yards to the ground, and the witch climbed up, as if it were a ladder.

In this way Rapunzel's lonely life went on for several years. The girl wasn't happy, but she wasn't exactly unhappy either.

One day, quite by chance, a young prince was riding in the woods when he heard a sweet voice carried on the air. It was Rapunzel, singing to keep herself company. Following the sound, he discovered the tall tower, but he could find no way inside and at last, discouraged, he rode home.

The prince could think of nothing except the beautiful voice and he returned day after day to listen to her singing.

As he stood in the shade of a tree one day, he saw a wizened old woman approach the tower and call out in a rusty voice:

"Rapunzel, Rapunzel, let down your hair."

Then a mass of golden hair tumbled down and the witch climbed up it.

"If that's the way to the sweet bird's nest," thought the prince, "I shall climb the ladder too."

The next day, around dusk, the prince called out:

"Rapunzel, Rapunzel, let down your hair,"

and the hair fell down like a waterfall, and the prince climbed up.

When she saw that her visitor was a young man, instead of the witch, Rapunzel was afraid. Locked away in her tower she knew nothing of men. But when the prince spoke softly and looked at her so gently, she knew she could trust him.

"Once I had heard your voice I couldn't rest until I saw you," he told her. "Now I cannot rest until you promise to marry me."

Rapunzel thought how handsome he was and how much happier she would be with him than with the witch. She took his hand and agreed to marry him.

But how would it be possible to escape, imprisoned as she was in this tower? She would weave a ladder, not of hair, but of silk, which the prince could bring, each time he visited her.

"Be sure to come at night," she told him. "The witch visits by day and she must never see you."

So the prince took care always to come at night, and that way the witch suspected nothing. But at last Rapunzel gave herself away.

"Why is it," she asked the witch one day, "that you are so much heavier to pull up than the prince? He climbs up in a . . ."

Too late! She could have bitten off her tongue.

"Oh, treacherous girl," screamed the witch. "You have deceived me."

She snatched up a pair of scissors in one hand and Rapunzel's beautiful hair in the other, and snip! snap! in a moment it lay on the floor.

Even then she showed no mercy. She turned the girl out of the tower and left her in a wild and desolate place to fend for herself as best she could.

Later that same day, when the prince came and called out:

"Rapunzel, Rapunzel, let down your hair,"

the witch cunningly tied the golden hair to the window hook and lowered it down.

The prince climbed up quickly and found, to his horror, not the sweet Rapunzel, but the wizened old woman looking at him with poisonous eyes.

"So you thought you could steal the songbird, did you? Well, the cat's got her and the cat'll get you too. She's gone, and you'll never see her again," she gloated.

Half mad with grief, the prince threw himself from the tower and would have died had he not landed in the thickest briars. But although he survived, thorns pierced his eyes and blinded him.

For many years he wandered through the woods living on whatever he could find, grieving for his lost wife, Rapunzel.

Eventually he wandered through the same wilderness where Rapunzel was living, with barely enough food for herself and the twins she had borne.

Just as he had done so long ago, the prince heard a sweet voice coming through the trees. It was a voice he knew, and he made his way towards it. Rapunzel saw him, and, recognising him, threw her arms around him, weeping tears of joy and sorrow. Two drops falling on his eyes healed them and restored his sight.

Then the two were united again and the prince took Rapunzel and their children back to his own kingdom. At last, they could all live happily ever after.

CINDERELLA

Imagine, if you can, a young girl whose mother died, leaving her to be brought up by her father. She was a pretty girl, with a kind nature exactly like her mother's, so father and daughter lived together very happily, until the day that he decided to marry again. But then everything changed.

This time the man chose a different type of wife entirely, the most conceited woman you ever saw, with a sharp tongue and a temper to match. Soon he was completely under her thumb.

The woman already had two daughters, unpleasant, spoilt creatures like herself, so she resented her stepdaughter's sweet nature and set out to make the girl's life as hard as she could.

This is how she did it. She gave her own daughters the best bedrooms and made her stepdaughter sleep in a draughty attic. She dressed her own daughters in fine clothes, while her stepdaughter's clothes were little more than rags. She left her own daughters to do as they pleased, which was usually nothing, but she made her stepdaughter work hard cleaning the house and waiting on her stepsisters.

To make matters worse, when her work was done, the only place the girl was allowed to rest was beside the fireplace, in among the cinders. And so she became known as Cinderella, the cinder girl.

But, despite all this, Cinderella grew more and more beautiful—

far more beautiful than her sisters with their fine clothes and fancy manners. And this made them even more envious of her.

Now, as it sometimes happened in those days, the king's son decided to hold a Grand Ball, and an invitation soon arrived for Cinderella's stepmother and her daughters. For the next week they talked of nothing else. They couldn't decide which clothes they

should choose, what hairstyle to have, which jewellery to wear, how to make up their faces—and this all made more work for Cinderella. Yet the harder she worked for them, the worse they treated her.

"Wouldn't you like to go with us?" they asked Cinderella.

"Oh, yes," she said. "If only I could."

"What a pity she can't," said one.

"Yes, it doesn't seem fair, does it?" said the other.

"Poor Cinderella," they said.

You might have thought they meant it, if you hadn't noticed how they smiled at one another, then burst out laughing, as if it was the most ridiculous suggestion in the world. Cinderella was used to their unkindness, but that didn't make it any easier to bear.

At last the important day arrived. When the rest of the family was ready they climbed into the carriage and Cinderella watched as they drove away. Then, alone in the house, she finally broke down and sobbed at the unfairness of life.

And it *was* unfair.

But one person cared about Cinderella and hated to see her upset, and that was her godmother. When she found the girl crying she said, "Oh, my dear, whatever's wrong?"

"I just wish . . . " Cinderella began. "If only I could go . . . " But she knew she couldn't. There was no point wishing for the impossible.

However, her godmother was a wise woman with fairy powers. She knew what Cinderella wished for, and nothing was impossible to her.

"You *can* go to the ball, if that's what you want. Do exactly as I tell you and we'll see what we can manage. Now, go into the garden and find me a pumpkin."

Cinderella went straight away, though she couldn't begin to see how a pumpkin was going to help. She brought back the largest she could find. Her godmother scooped out the middle, then touched it lightly with a magic wand.

Only a tap, the slightest touch, nothing much, and it became an elegant coach, covered with gold.

"Well, that's a start," said her godmother. "But a coach without horses won't go far. Bring me the mousetrap."

Again Cinderella did as she was told. Inside were six grey mice. She lifted the trap door. One by one the mice ran out. But once more her godmother was ready with her wand.

Only a tap, the slightest touch, nothing much, and the mice turned into six fine horses, harnessed and ready to go.

"A coach without a coachman isn't a great deal of use," said her godmother, looking around as if she expected to find one in the kitchen.

"The rat trap!" suggested Cinderella. In it they found a big fat rat with long whiskers.

Another tap, only a touch, and he changed into an amiable coachman, without a sign of a tail.

"Better and better," said her godmother. "Now, into the garden again. You'll find six lizards hiding behind the watering can. Bring them to me."

Cinderella brought them in.

A tap and a touch and six smart footmen in gold livery jumped up behind the coach just as if they'd been doing it all their lives.

"Now," said her godmother, "are you ready to go?"

Cinderella looked down at her clothes. She hated to seem ungrateful but she could hardly go to a ball dressed like this.

The lightest tap, the gentlest touch, and she was dressed in a gown of gold and silver. The slippers which stood ready for her to wear were made of glass, sparkling crystal. There has never been a pair to match them. Cinderella put them on. A perfect fit.

Looking exactly like a princess, she stepped into the coach.

But her godmother had one more thing to say. "Promise me you will leave the ball before midnight. One moment after twelve and your coach, horses, coachman and clothes will disappear. You'll be just as you were."

"I promise," said Cinderella. "I won't forget." It seemed to her a small price to pay. She thanked her godmother and waved goodbye.

When Cinderella reached the palace, her arrival was announced and the king's son himself came out to meet her. As he led her into the ballroom, the music and dancing stopped. The prince and Cinderella began to dance. She looked so graceful that at first all the other guests sat and watched.

"Who is she?" everyone wanted to know.

"Certainly a princess," they whispered.

The whole evening she danced only with the prince; he wasn't interested in anyone else.

At supper she sat close by her sisters and once or twice spoke to them. They were very flattered and answered her politely. They didn't recognise her: people usually see what they expect to see, and they hardly expected to see their own sister dancing with the prince.

All too soon the clock struck quarter to twelve. Cinderella remembered her promise. She curtsied and left.

When she reached home, Cinderella told her godmother all about the ball and asked if she could go again the next night. The prince had begged her to come. As they were talking, Cinderella heard her sisters arrive home. She hurried to let them in.

"It's very late," she said, yawning and rubbing her eyes, as if she'd been asleep.

"You wouldn't have noticed if you'd been with us," they said. "We've had the most wonderful time. A beautiful princess came to the ball. She spent almost the whole evening talking to *us*."

"Who was she?" asked Cinderella.

"Nobody knows, but the prince is desperate to find out. You should have seen her clothes . . . "

"I wish I had," said Cinderella. "Perhaps tomorrow I could go too."

"You! Whatever would you wear?"

"I could borrow a dress from you," she suggested.

"Lend a dress to a cindergirl? Don't be ridiculous," they said.

They were quite sure she must be joking, as of course she was. Cinderella didn't need *their* help.

The next day, as soon as her sisters had left, Cinderella began to get ready. This time she wore a dress of deep blue silk, covered in jewels that sparkled like stars in the night sky. And again she wore her glass slippers.

The prince was waiting for her when she arrived. Throughout the evening he didn't leave her side. He was determined she wouldn't slip away from him again.

Cinderella was so happy and excited that she didn't once think about the time. That's how easily promises are forgotten. Before she could believe it, the clock began to strike midnight.

One! Two! Three! In panic Cinderella fled from the ballroom.

Four! Five! Six! She ran down the steep staircase. She could hear voices and footsteps, but she didn't dare to look back.

Seven! Eight! Nine! Running across the courtyard she stumbled and lost one of her glass slippers, but there was no time to stop.

Ten! Eleven! *Twelve*! By the time Cinderella was clear of the palace she was again dressed in rags. All the magic had vanished, all except one of her glass slippers. She took it off and hid it safely in her pocket.

The prince had tried to follow Cinderella, but he couldn't catch her. He only found her other glass slipper, lying on the ground. He

questioned the palace guards; she must have passed them. But they said they'd seen no one. They didn't imagine the prince would be interested in a poor kitchen girl dressed in rags.

Cinderella reached home just in time to open the door to her sisters as they returned from the ball. She asked them if the beautiful princess had come again.

"Well, she did," they told her, "but the moment it struck midnight she disappeared. She ran off into the night, with the prince chasing after her."

"He came back clutching her slipper," said one.

"Obviously madly in love," said the other.

"Do you really think so?" Cinderella asked.

"Oh, yes," they both agreed. There was no doubt about it.

And they were right. The very next day the prince announced that he would marry the girl whose foot fitted the glass slipper.

First it was tried on by all the princesses, then the duchesses, then all the ladies of the court. You should have seen the variety of feet. Some had big feet and some had small feet, but none were small enough to fit the tiny slipper. So that was a mystery.

Then it was taken into every home in the land. At last it was the turn of Cinderella's sisters to try it on.

Well, they squeezed and they squashed their feet to get the slipper on. They pushed and they pulled until their fingers ached. They trapped their toes and hurt their heels and made them bleed, but it was no use. They had to give it up.

By now the prince was beginning to lose all hope.

"Isn't there anyone else in the house?" he asked.

"No other *lady*," they said. "There's Cinderella, but she doesn't count."

Immediately the sisters wished they'd held their tongues, because the prince insisted they bring Cinderella and let her try it on.

The moment she sat down and took the slipper, they saw how easily it slipped on, how perfectly it fitted. And when she took from her pocket the matching slipper and put that on too, they were speechless.

The prince recognised her, even in her rags. And when her godmother appeared and once more, with only a tap, the slightest touch, transformed Cinderella's clothes, even her sisters saw that she was the beautiful princess from the ball.

Then they were afraid, and regretted how they had treated her.

"Do forgive us," they begged her. "We're truly sorry."

Cinderella did forgive them, because that was her nature. And soon after, when she married the prince, she took her sisters to live at court, where they met two great lords. These two were an equally proud and unpleasant pair, so when they married they made a good match. All four of them lived miserably together for many long years.

But as for Cinderella and the prince, now they lived happily ever after, which was exactly what they deserved.

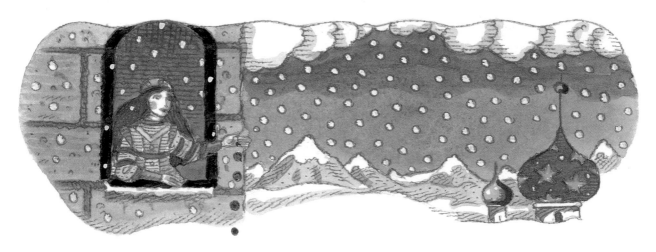

SNOW WHITE

It was the middle of winter, a long time ago, and a young queen sat sewing by an open window. As she looked up, watching the snow fall like feathers from the sky, she pricked herself, and three drops of blood fell from her finger. The red of her blood, on the white of the snow, framed by the black of the window, was so striking that the queen made a wish that she would have a child as white as snow, as red as blood and as black as the ebony wood of the window frame.

And in time her wish came true; she gave birth to a little girl with snow-white skin, blood-red lips and hair as black as ebony, and they named her Snow White. But when the child was born the young queen died, so joy and sorrow cancelled each other out.

In less than a year the king took a second wife, as beautiful as the first—no, even more beautiful. But she was so vain. The only way she could be happy was in knowing that she was the most beautiful woman in the kingdom.

Now, how could she know this? Because she had a magic mirror, and whenever she stood in front of it she said,

"Mirror, mirror, on the wall,
Who is the fairest one of all?"

And the mirror answered,

"Queen, you are the fairest one of all."

Then she was happy because she knew that the mirror always told the truth.

But nothing stays the same. The years passed and Snow White grew more and more beautiful, as sweet and fresh as the air on a spring morning, and how could the queen compete with that?

The day came when she stood in front of her mirror and asked,

"Mirror, mirror, on the wall,
Who is the fairest one of all?"

And the mirror answered,

"Queen, you were *the fairest, 'tis true,*
But Snow White's a thousand times lovelier than you."

From that moment on, every time the queen looked at Snow White she resented her more. And the resentment turned into hatred which soon had the queen in its power. She couldn't rest until she was rid of the girl, so she called her huntsman to her and said, "Take Snow White into the deepest wood and kill her. I never want to set eyes on her again." And, because she wanted to be sure he had done it, she told him to bring back Snow White's heart.

The huntsman was honest and loyal to the queen, but he couldn't bear to think of killing the girl. When Snow White begged him to spare her life he was glad to do it. He knew she wouldn't survive in the woods for long, without food or shelter, but at least his own conscience would be clear.

To satisfy the queen, the huntsman captured a wild boar and took back its heart and the wicked woman ate it, thinking she was devouring her enemy. That's how much she hated Snow White.

Meanwhile Snow White hurried ever deeper into the wood. By evening, she was completely lost.

At last she came to a cottage. Inside everything was neat and welcoming. A table with a snow-white cloth was set for seven people, food and drink already waiting at each place. And along one wall were seven little beds, covered with snow-white quilts. By now Snow White was so hungry and so tired that she couldn't resist taking just a mouthful from each plate and a sip from each cup. Then she tried to decide which bed to lie on. But each bed in turn was unsuitable: it was either too long or too short, too high or too low, too hard or too soft, until she tried the seventh bed, which was just right. She lay down on it and fell asleep, safe at last.

Some time later the owners of the house returned, seven dwarfs who worked all day mining for gold in the mountains. They could soon tell that they had had a visitor; things weren't exactly as they'd left them.

"Someone's been sitting on my chair," said the first.

"Someone's been eating my food," said the second.

"Someone's been drinking my wine," said the third.

"Someone's been using my knife," said the fourth.

"And my fork," said the fifth.

"And my spoon," said the sixth.

"Someone's been meddling with my things too," said the seventh.

Then the first dwarf noticed that someone had been lying on his bed, because the quilt was creased. Soon each of them found that his quilt had been lain on. But the seventh found that his was *still* being lain on. There was Snow White fast asleep on his bed.

The other dwarfs crowded around her. She looked so sweet and comfortable that they hadn't the heart to disturb her. They left her to sleep in peace, and the seventh dwarf spent an hour with each of the others throughout the night.

In the morning, when Snow White woke, she was afraid, but the dwarfs soon reassured her. She told them everything that had happened to her.

"You can stay with us," they said. "If you'll clean our house, cook our meals, wash and mend our clothes, we'll protect you."

But during the day while they were at work, Snow White would be alone in the house. Then she would have to be careful.

"The queen will soon find out where you are," they warned her. "Don't let anyone in." And Snow White promised them she wouldn't.

For a while, the queen felt secure that she was now the most beautiful. But one day she again stood in front of her glass and said,

"Mirror, mirror, on the wall,
Who is the fairest one of all?"

And the mirror answered,

"Queen, you are fairer than most, 'tis true,
But over the hills where the seven dwarfs dwell
Snow White is still alive and well,
And she's a thousand times lovelier than you."

Imagine, if you can, the queen's temper. She was dizzy with rage. The wretched girl was still alive, so the huntsman had failed her. This time she would do the job herself. She stained her face and disguised herself as a pedlar. Then she made the journey to the place where the dwarfs lived.

"Silks for sale. Ribbons and lovely laces," she called.

Snow White looked out and saw the fine things the pedlar had to sell.

"Surely it wouldn't hurt to look at the old woman's things," she thought. She unlocked the door and chose the prettiest of the laces.

"Here, let me thread it for you," the old woman offered.

Then, with fast fingers, she laced Snow White's bodice firm and tight, so tight that the girl couldn't breathe, and fell unconscious to the floor.

When the dwarfs returned that night and discovered her lying there they soon found the cause. They cut the laces and Snow White began to breathe. Then she told them about the pedlar woman.

"It was the queen, depend upon it. And she'll be back," they told her. "You must open the door to no one." And Snow White promised.

So, for a while, all was well, until the next time the queen stood in front of her mirror. Again she said,

"Mirror, mirror, on the wall,
Who is the fairest one of all?"

And again the mirror answered,

"Queen, you are fairer than most, 'tis true,
But over the hills where the seven dwarfs dwell
Snow White is still alive and well,
And she's a thousand times lovelier than you."

Then the queen herself could scarcely breathe for anger. This time she would have to plan more carefully. She made a poisoned comb, cleverly carved and inlaid with mother-of-pearl, certain to catch the eye. She took on a different disguise and travelled over the hills to the dwarfs' cottage.

"Come and buy," she called. "Come and buy."

Once more Snow White looked out. This time she said, "I can't open the door. I'm not allowed to."

"There's no need," said the woman. "But it doesn't hurt to look."

She held out the tantalising comb and Snow White *had* to have it. Snow White opened the door and bought it from her.

"Here, let me comb your lovely hair," said the woman.

No sooner did the comb sink into Snow White's hair than the poison set to work, and she fell senseless to the ground.

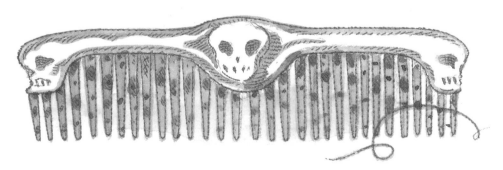

It was fortunate that the dwarfs came home quite soon and discovered the comb. Once they'd removed it she began to recover.

"This time you were lucky," they told her. "Take no more chances. Don't speak to anyone." And again Snow White promised.

When the queen returned to her castle she went straight to her mirror. Picture her fury when the mirror gave her the same answer a third time. She swore then that she would kill Snow White, even if it cost her own life. She locked herself in a secret room where she prepared a poisoned apple. It looked so tasty that it was impossible to resist, but was so deadly that one bite could kill.

This time she pretended to be a farmer's wife. She made her way to the dwarfs' cottage and knocked at the door.

Snow White looked out and said, "I'm sorry, I can't let you in."

"Don't fret," said the farmer's wife. "It makes no difference to me. Here, have an apple anyway." And she held one out.

When she saw the perfect apple, Snow White was tempted, but she shook her head. "No, I can't. I mustn't."

"What *are* you afraid of? Do you think I might poison you?" the woman laughed. "Look, I'll cut it in half and share it with you."

Now, this apple was so cunningly made that only the red half was poisoned. The old woman handed it to Snow White and started to eat the green half herself. Then Snow White felt sure it must be safe, and she took it greedily. But the moment she bit into the apple, she fell dead on the floor.

"White as snow, red as blood, black as ebony! Nothing can save you now," cried the queen.

And at long last, when she returned to the palace and stood in front of her mirror, it told her what she wanted to hear.

 *"Queen, you are the fairest one of all."*

The queen shuddered with pleasure. Now she was satisfied, as far as a jealous heart can ever be satisfied.

When the dwarfs came home that evening they found Snow White lying dead on the ground. And this time she *was* dead. Although they tried to revive her, they couldn't do it.

For three days they mourned her and wept over her, and finally they came to bury her. But she still looked so fresh and beautiful that the thought of covering her with earth and hiding her away seemed wrong. Instead they made her a glass coffin, with her name and an inscription saying that she was a king's daughter. They set it high on the hillside and each took turns to guard her. Even the animals and birds came and wept for her.

Time passed, and Snow White continued to look as if she were only sleeping. Then one day a young prince, travelling close by, came upon the dwarfs' cottage. When he saw Snow White in her coffin he was so moved by her that he asked the dwarfs if he could take her away with him.

"Not for all the gold in the world," they said.

But the prince told them that now he had seen her, he couldn't live without her, and begged them again. At last, out of pity for him, they agreed. But as his servants lifted the coffin they stumbled and almost dropped it. The apple dislodged itself from her throat, and suddenly Snow White came back to life.

The prince told her who he was and how much he loved her. He asked her to marry him and return with him to his father's kingdom. And Snow White had only to look on him to love him too.

The marriage was arranged and everyone was invited, including Snow White's stepmother, the wicked queen.

Dressed in her finest clothes, she stood in front of her mirror and said,

"Mirror, mirror, on the wall,
Who is the fairest one of all?"

And the mirror answered,

> *"Queen, you are fairer than most, 'tis true,*
> *But the new queen's even lovelier than you."*

What could it mean? The queen's heart was fit to burst with anger. First she was desperate to go, then she couldn't bear to go, then she couldn't bear *not* to go. She *had* to see who this new queen was. And when she saw it was Snow White she was fixed to the spot with fear and horror.

But red hot iron slippers had been prepared as her punishment, and the wicked woman danced in them until she was dead.

THE THREE WISHES

One night a man and his wife were sitting before their fire, talking, cosy-like. She was a good wife and he was a good man so they were passing happy, most of the time. But now and again the pair of them couldn't help feeling just a bit envious of their neighbours, who were richer than them.

"It don't seem fair," said the wife.

"It certainly don't," said her husband.

"Now, if I had a wish," said she, "I know just what I'd do with it. Ooh, I'd be happier than all of 'em."

"And me," said the man. "Pity there isn't such a thing as a fairy, right here, this minute."

And suddenly there was, right there, that minute, in their own kitchen. All shining and smiling.

"You can have three wishes," the fairy told them, "but take care, once they're gone, that's it, there'll be no more." And then she disappeared. She was very business-like.

Well, the couple were amazed. They felt as if they had their heads on back to front.

"Whatever d'you make of that?" said he.

"I'll tell you what I make of it," said she. "I know fine well what I'll wish for—not that I'm wishing yet," she said, quick as a flash, in case the fairy was listening, "but, if I *were*, I should want to be handsome, rich and famous."

"Where's the use in that?" said he. "That won't stop you being sick and miserable or dying young. Far better be healthy and hopeful and live to be a hundred."

"And how would that help, if you were poor and hungry in the meantime?" said she. "Just prolonging the misery, in my opinion."

Well, her husband had to agree with that.

"Hmmm," said he. "This is going to need some thinking about. I reckon we'd best go to bed and sleep on it. We'll be wiser in the morning than the evening."

"True enough," said his wife.

But the fire was still burning up brightly, so they sat on a little longer, talking things over, cosy-like.

They were feeling that happy.

"It'd be a waste to leave this nice fire," said the man.

"It does seem a pity, though," said she, "we've nowt to cook on it. I wish we had a dozen sausages for our supper."

Uh, oh! No sooner said than done.

Down the chimney fell a long chain of sausages and landed at their feet. And that was one wish gone.

The man was flummoxed. He could hardly speak for rage.

"A dozen sausages! What a witless woman is my wife. Of all the harebrained individuals . . . I wish the dozen sausages were stuck on the end of your nose, you nincompoop."

Uh, oh! No sooner said than done.

The sausages leapt up on to the end of the wife's nose and hung there like an elephant's trunk. And that was two wishes gone.

"Oh, flipping heck, what have you done to me!" said she. She took hold of the sausages and tried to get them off. She pulled and pummelled them, she twisted and turned them, but they wouldn't budge. In sheer temper she jumped out of her chair, stepped on the end of them and almost tripped up. By now she was fizzing mad!

Her husband sat there open-mouthed, just watching.

"Don't sit there gawping, you owl, do something, for goodness sake," she cried.

So then the husband tried too. He grabbed hold of the sausages and he pulled and he pulled. It was a regular tug-of-war. But the sausages just stretched longer and longer and longer. When he finally let go they sprang back like a piece of elastic, boxing his wife round the ears—biff! biff! biff! Then they hung down, long and floppy again.

"Oh, what a wretched woman I am," she began to cry. "Whatever will I do?" And her tears ran down the sausages.

"Don't fret," said he. "I know just what to do. We must use our last wish to make ourselves very rich. Then I shall have the smartest gold case in the world made for you to wear over the sausages. Maybe a matching crown. You'll look very grand."

"Are you a complete idiot?" said the wife. "Have you totally lost your senses? D'you suppose I want to spend the rest of my days trailing sausages on the end of my nose? You must have a screw loose. I want that last wish to get rid of these sausages," she said, "or . . . I shall throw myself out of the window."

And to show she meant it, she rushed across the room, threw open the window and jumped up on the window-sill.

Then her husband couldn't help but smile. The sight of his poor wife, standing on the window-sill with a string of sausages hanging from her nose, was such a comical sight. And, after all, they were still sitting downstairs, so she hardly had far to jump.

But he was a bit of a tease and he couldn't resist winding her up one last time.

"Of course, my dear, you must do whatever you think best, but it does seem a pity, knowing as how you wanted to be famous and all that. And truly, the more I look at it, the more it grows on me. I'm really beginning to think as it suits you."

"Suits me? A nose as long as a skipping rope? I should be tripping over it every way I turned," she cried.

"Happen you could wrap it round your neck, lovely, then it'd serve as a scarf an'all," he said, trying to be helpful.

At this, his wife was fit to explode, but the man couldn't keep it up a minute longer. He started to grin, so he got up and helped her off the ledge. For he did truly love her.

"I wish my wife could have her nose back to normal," he said.

Da daa! No sooner said than done.

The sausages fell to the floor and coiled themselves up like a pet snake.

"Well, some good's come of the bad," said she, "at least we still have the sausages."

"I'll build up the fire," said he.

"I'll put on the pan," said she.

"What a good idea," said he.

So that's what they did.

The pair of them sat late into the night, frying sausages and toasting their toes before the fire, and talking, cosy-like.

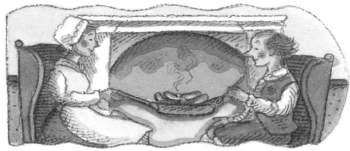

THE SOMETIMES RUDE
HISTORY OF TOM THUMB

Now, I hope you're sitting comfortably. This is a *long* story about a *short* fellow by the name of Tom Thumb—so called because he was no bigger than a man's thumb. But don't imagine that meant he never travelled very far. He was a brave lad whose adventures took him a great distance. He flew for miles in a raven's beak, went swimming downriver inside a fish, fell down a giant's chimney. Let me tell you, the lad found himself in some strange places: hiding in a mousehole, trapped inside a cow's stomach and, one time, almost cooked in the middle of a steamed pudding. But let's slow down and start again—at the beginning this time.

IN WHICH TOM IS BORN AND GETS HIS NAME

Once upon a time, in the days of King Arthur, there lived an old couple, a ploughman and his wife. In every respect they were as happy as the day is long, except for the fact that they had no children.

"Our house is too quiet. I wish we had a little 'un to liven us up," said the man.

"Aye, no matter how small he was," agreed his wife. "I'd be content if he were no bigger than your thumb."

Well, it didn't seem a lot to ask, so that decided the old man. He would go and see Merlin, the famous wizard, and get his advice.

"If only you could help us, sir. We'd be happy with a child the size of my thumb."

That's what he asked for and that's what he got.

By the time the man reached home, his wife had given birth to a baby boy, not much bigger than a tadpole. Then, before their very eyes, in the space of four minutes, the baby grew into a child—the exact size of his father's thumb. What do you think of that?

The old couple thought it was wonderful. They set about making all the miniature furniture he would need. But first he must be christened.

"What shall we call him?" said the man.

"Tom," said his wife, who'd already given it some thought.

"Thumb," said her husband, for obvious reasons.

So Tom Thumb he was called.

The Queen of the Fairies came to the christening and offered to be his godmother, which was useful because she gave him some fairy powers. But best of all she brought him a wonderful suit of clothes. He looked a picture.

An oak-leaf hat upon his head,
For a plume, a tittimouse tail.
His shirt spun from a spider's web,
Made perfectly to scale.
His coat was woven thistledown;
His trousers blue-tit's feathers;
Stockings made from apple rinds,
And boots of mouse-skin leather.

As long as he lived, Tom Thumb never grew another inch. He was little, there's no denying that, but more to the point he was a little terror.

IN WHICH TOM ISN'T ENTIRELY HONEST, AND GETS INTO TROUBLE WITH HIS FRIENDS

In one way Tom Thumb was the same as other boys; he liked to play out with his friends. In all their games, Tom always won. How was it, the other boys wondered, that no sooner was Tom out of the game than back he came with another counter to play with, another marble to roll, another cherry stone to throw? I'll tell you how: whenever Tom lost, he simply climbed into someone else's pocket and stole what he needed to get back into the game.

But one day he was careless. One of his friends found Tom Thumb climbing out of *his* bag of treasures. Tom was struggling with an acorn the size of his head.

"Now I've caught you," said his friend. "Back you go and stay there." And he pulled the string tight round Tom's waist so that he was caught, half in and half out.

"Let me go," shouted Tom, his little legs waving helplessly in the air.

"I will not," said his friend. And he swung the bag round his finger until Tom was quite dizzy.

Tom set up such a commotion that his mother heard his cries and came running into the street.

"You put him down," she ordered. "You big bully!"

She was just like all mothers; she doted on her little boy. In her eyes Tom Thumb could do no wrong. His friends, however, enjoyed teaching him a lesson. But Tom soon got his own back: then those boys were sorry.

IN WHICH TOM THUMB GETS HIS REVENGE
⤶ AND THOSE BOYS *ARE* SORRY ⤷

One day at school, Tom saw a sunbeam stretching across the classroom. It looked for all the world like a washing line. And that gave him a fine idea. With the fairy powers he was given as a baby, he hung a row of his mother's best glasses and pots along the sunbeam, just as if they were clothes hanging out to dry.

"Now, my clever friends," said Tom, "let's see you do that."

Well, if he could do it so could they. One by one they carried in their mothers' best vases and dishes. In no time—*smash! crash! bang!*—the room was ankle deep in broken glass and china. Then they were in trouble and no mistake. Those boys couldn't sit down for a week.

> *If they'd been as clever*
> *As our hero Tom Thumb,*
> *They wouldn't have suffered*
> *The cane on their bum.*
> *Ouch!*

Tom laughed, but he didn't laugh for long. He was sent home and told not to come back until he could behave better. Even at home, under his mother's nose, Tom was soon in trouble again. Much worse trouble this time.

IN WHICH TOM FALLS INTO THE PUDDING MIX
AND NEARLY GETS COOKED

Tom was such an inquisitive boy. He always had his nose into something. One day he was perched on top of the salt cellar, on the kitchen table, watching his mother making the mixture for a steamed pudding. She only left him for a moment, while she fetched some milk, but he climbed up the side of the bowl to have a closer look—a taste, more likely. Suddenly he slipped. Over the edge he went, sliding down into the mixture, glug, glug, glug. All the way to the bottom.

Tom's mother was so busy that she didn't even miss him. In no time she'd turned the mixture into a pudding bag and put it in the pan to boil.

Poor Tom! He was full of pudding: his ears, his eyes, his nose and his mouth, so he couldn't shout for help. Soon he felt the water beginning to boil. He jumped up and down. He struggled and he strained. He kicked and he clouted that pudding until it danced in the pan. Tom's mother watched it; her eyes grew round.

"Oh, heaven save us. The pudding's bewitched," she cried.

Next moment the pudding almost leaped out of the pan on its own.

"Help! Help!" cried Tom's mother.

She lifted the pudding bag out of the pan and, in terror, flung it through the open window. It landed at the feet of a passing tinker.

"Well, I'll be blessed," he said. It wasn't every day that steamed puddings rained from the sky. He picked it up and ran off with it, before anyone could claim it back.

When he thought it was safe to stop, the tinker sat down under a tree, holding the precious pudding. He paused for a moment to enjoy the anticipation of that thick, fruity mixture. He licked his lips.

Imagine his horror when the pudding nearly jumped off his knee! It bounced up and down as if it was alive and began to make strange noises.

"Globablobalob. Blubalubalub . . . "

The tinker dropped it and ran off down the road. He ran as though he expected the pudding to follow him and eat *him* up instead.

Left there on the grass, Tom finally managed to free himself and made his sticky way home, still covered in pudding. His mother, who was so glad to have him back, bathed him in a teacup, dried him with a handkerchief and put him to bed.

"I hope that has taught you a lesson," she said.

But of course it hadn't.

IN WHICH TOM IS EATEN BY A COW AND COMES
TO A STICKY END! UGH!

Shortly after that Tom had another adventure. His mother used to take him with her when she went to the field to do the milking. On windy days she left him tied by a long string to a thistle, in case he should blow away. But Tom, curious as ever, wandered off one day and began to explore. He soon ventured under the nose of the cow that his mother had just finished milking. In one mouthful the cow ate him up, string, thistle and all. It was only by sheer luck that she swallowed him down in one piece.

So there was Tom, inside the cow's stomach. Raining down on top of him came more and more thistles and grass. Tom started thumping and jumping up and down.

"No more food," he cried. "No more food."

The cow broke out in the most pathetic mooing. But Tom still kept up his dancing. It must have felt as if a miniature football team were playing inside her.

When she had finished her milking, his mother came looking for Tom, but there was no sign of him.

"Tom, Tom, where are you?" she called.

"I'm here, mother, in the cow's stomach," came a very small voice, "and I don't like it."

Then Tom's mother raced home and brought back the biggest bottle of medicine you ever saw. She opened the cow's mouth and poured it down, soaking Tom in the process.

And it worked; Tom was out in no time. Of course, he had to come out one end or the other, and neither of them would have been very pleasant. But, in this case, it was the worse of the two . . . in the middle of a huge cow pat, I'm sorry to say.

"Phew!" said his father, holding his nose.

It was several baths later before Tom smelt sweet again.

"Surely *that* will teach him a lesson," his father said.

But of course it didn't.

IN WHICH TOM GOES FLYING AND DOESN'T ⊱ COME BACK ⊰

Sometimes Tom liked to go with his father into the fields when he was ploughing. Then he had to be careful. The furrows were so deep that if he fell into them Tom couldn't easily climb out. But he was a brave boy and he liked to be helpful.

One day his father set Tom to scare off the crows. He armed himself with an ear of barley, which was like a huge cudgel to him, and waved it in the air.

"Shoo, crows," shouted Tom Thumb. "Be off, or I'll put you in a pie."

But one time a raven swooped down and picked Tom up, along with the ear of barley, and carried him in his beak for miles.

Tom's father watched his son disappear, until he was only a speck in the sky. For weeks after, he and his wife climbed trees and church towers, searching every nest and hidey-hole they could find, but they never discovered a sign of their son.

This time he really was lost.

IN WHICH TOM FALLS FROM A GREAT HEIGHT AND NARROWLY ESCAPES A GIANT

Meanwhile Tom Thumb, our brave hero, was travelling over forests and mountains. All the time he was carried in the raven's beak, he kept on crying out, "Shoo, bird, shoo, shoo."

Tom wriggled and jiggled around so that the raven almost dropped him. Consequently the bird was soon tired out and stopped to rest on the tallest point of a very tall castle—the castle of an infamous giant—and finally let him go.

Tom found himself looking down a tall chimney. Beneath him he could hear the sounds of the giant snapping and cracking the bones of his victims and smacking his horrible lips.

Tom Thumb was frozen with terror, but that very moment a gust of wind lifted him up and carried him tumbling down the chimney. He landed at the feet of the giant, who gave chase and tried to catch him.

The brave lad dodged and darted between his legs so that the clumsy giant could never get a grip on him. Finally Tom escaped by scuttling into a mousehole. The giant poked sticks into the hole and shouted terrible oaths about what he would do if he got hold of Tom. But he couldn't get Tom out, so he went off to bed in a rare old temper.

In the middle of the night, Tom woke to hear the heavy tread of the giant, the swing of his huge club, and his deep voice roaring:

"Fi, fee, fo, fan,
I smell the blood of an Englishman.
Be he alive, or be he dead,
I'll grind his bones to make my bread."

Tom sat tight, but he knew he couldn't stay in that dark little mousehole for ever. He would have to face the giant and take his chances. So that's what the brave boy did.

IN WHICH TOM SERVES THE GIANT BUT LEARNS THAT GIANTS AREN'T TO BE TRUSTED

Tom Thumb slipped out of the mousehole and spoke up in as loud a voice as he could manage.

"Here I am, hardly a mouthful for the likes of you. Why don't you let me work for you instead? Being so small must make me useful for something."

Well, that was true enough. The giant, who had no cat, set him to catch mice in the castle, clean cobwebs in awkward corners and serve as a key to unlock the castle doors. There were all manner of little jobs he could do, and Tom Thumb did them well.

But giants are not to be trusted, and neither was this one.

One day Tom was busy turning the giant's meat before the fire, holding up a spoon to keep the heat off his face. The giant crept up behind him, snatched hold of him, and held Tom up close to his huge and horrible face.

Quick as a flash, Tom jumped into the giant's mouth and slid down his throat into his belly. Then he gave that giant a good kicking. He raced around punching and pummelling him, until the giant thought he had swallowed the devil and half his family.

When he could stand it no longer, the giant raced up to the top of his castle and was sick over the battlements. So this time Tom came out the other end—and that wasn't a lot better! Into the river he fell and it carried him swiftly away.

IN WHICH TOM IS SWALLOWED *AGAIN* AND SURVIVES TO TELL THE TALE

Now, as if he hadn't already had enough trouble, Tom Thumb was soon swallowed *again*, by a huge fish, which carried him even further. It would have carried him out to sea, had it not been caught itself by a fisherman.

When the fisherman saw the great catch he had made, he took the fish as a present to the court of King Arthur, where it was delivered to the royal kitchen.

The cook, with one quick slice, opened it up. Out came our hero, wet but otherwise none the worse for his adventure.

"Who'd have believed it," said the cook. "This'll make a fine surprise for the king."

When Tom Thumb was finally brought before King Arthur, he was disguised inside a mutton pie. Just as it was about to be served, up he popped, which made the king and all his court roar with laughter.

"Tom Thumb, Your Majesty. At your service!"

Then Tom Thumb had a few tales to tell. He told them in such a lively manner that he soon became the king's favourite and lived a long and happy life at court.

EPILOGUE

Tom Thumb's adventures continued for years:
More giants, more frights, more attacks,
A new set of clothes, a coach drawn by mice,
And a ride on a butterfly's back.

Bearing a sixpence, for two days and nights,
He returned to the place he was born.
His parents, delighted to see him again,
Fed him walnuts, and whitebait and prawn.

But whatever became of this miniature boy?
What was his final mishap?
After fighting most bravely, a spider's cruel bite
Put an end to the marvellous chap.

So wipe your eye, now bow your head,
For brave Tom Thumb is dead.

THE SLEEPING BEAUTY

In the days when there were still fairies, there lived a king and queen who were immensely rich. They lived in a magnificent castle with servants, golden coaches, and everything that money could buy, so they should have been happy, but they weren't. All the money in the world couldn't buy what *they* wanted: a child of their own.

One day, when the queen was walking beside the castle, she found a fish on the riverbank. It had thrown itself completely out of the water and lay gasping and close to death. She quickly lifted it back into the river and so saved its life. In return the fish told the queen, "Within a year your dearest wish will come true." And sure enough, as the fish had promised, the queen gave birth to a baby girl.

When the child was born the king was the happiest man alive. He held a great feast to celebrate and decided to invite all those fairies who lived in the kingdom. Now the fact was, the king only owned twelve gold plates and there were thirteen fairies, so he was forced to leave one out. This proved unlucky for the king, as you will see.

After the feast the fairies gathered around the child's cradle. Each gave her a gift; beauty, wisdom, grace and many other virtues. Finally it was the turn of the twelfth fairy. But before she had time to speak, the doors of the castle flew open and in came the thirteenth fairy—the one who'd been neglected. She was dressed entirely in black and was in such a rage that everyone shrank back in fear as she passed.

Standing before the child's cradle, the fairy cried out, "Since you chose to ignore me, this will be my gift: when the princess is fifteen she will pierce her finger with a spindle and drop down dead." Then the fairy turned her back on the baby and left without another word.

The king and queen looked all around in despair, but no one knew how to console them. But the twelfth fairy, who still had to speak, offered them some hope.

"Although I cannot undo the curse," she said, "at least I can soften it. The princess will not die, only sleep for a hundred years."

A hundred years! This was small comfort to the king. He was determined to protect his daughter if he possibly could. He made a law banning the use of spindles throughout the kingdom, and he ordered that those which already existed should be burned. Only then did the king and queen feel secure.

Over the years all the other gifts were fulfilled. The princess grew up beautiful and good, just as the fairies had promised, so that whoever met her couldn't help but love her.

One day, when the princess was fifteen, while the king and queen were out riding, she began to explore parts of the castle into which she'd never been allowed. She discovered a derelict tower, and climbed the winding staircase to the very top. There she found a door; in the lock was a golden key. She turned it and the door opened to reveal an old woman sitting, spinning flax.

"What are you doing?" asked the princess, because of course she'd never seen a spinning wheel in her life.

"Spinning," said the old woman. "Here, you try." And she handed her the spindle.

The instant the princess touched it she pricked her finger and three drops of blood appeared. She fell into a deep sleep.

Very soon the king and queen returned from riding, followed by their servants, and the enchantment descended on the castle like a fine mist.

One moment life was going on as normal. The kitchen maid stirred the soup and the butler poured wine for the king's dinner. The kitchen boy, turning the spit to roast the meat, stole a tempting scrap for himself, and the cook, catching him in the act, reached out to cuff his ear. But the next moment they all stopped—just like that—and fell asleep where they stood. Even the fire over which the meat was cooking died down and seemed to rest.

No one escaped, not even the animals: the horses steaming in the stables, the dogs fighting in the courtyard, the doves cooing on the castle roof, the flies resting on the kitchen walls—all suddenly fell asleep and everywhere was silent and still.

Around the castle a hedge of thorns appeared, deep and impassable, and so high that only the tallest turret could be seen above it. It wrapped itself around the sleepers like a thick blanket, keeping everyone inside safe and undisturbed.

For years afterwards stories of a beautiful princess who lay sleeping inside the castle were often repeated. A succession of young men came from distant countries hoping to find a way inside, but the hedge always defeated them. No matter how fiercely they fought a way through, the hedge always grew back again, thicker and sharper, catching them in its thorns. Many of them lost their lives in the struggle.

But one day a king's son was travelling through the kingdom and was told the story by an old man who lived nearby.

Immediately the prince knew that he too must try. The old man reminded him of all the others who had been equally convinced they could succeed, but had nevertheless perished in the thorns. But the young man was determined.

Now it happened that the hundred years came to an end on that very day. As the prince approached the hedge, it parted magically before him and offered a clear way through, then closed again behind him.

The king's son walked on until he came to the courtyard, but there he almost gave up at the sight of so many lifeless bodies. The silence was unbroken even by the buzz of a fly; the still air unruffled by the slightest breeze. Such a strange atmosphere made him almost lose his nerve, but he made himself go on. As he came closer, he could see that these were not dead, but sleeping bodies, overcome in the middle of their daily business. Some snored gently, others smiled as if dreaming pleasant dreams.

The young man made his way through the kitchens and came into the great hall where the king and queen sat side by side on their thrones, heads bowed to one another, also sound asleep.

And still he kept on and at last came to the top of the tall tower where the Sleeping Beauty lay. When he looked down on her and saw that she was as beautiful as he had heard, and even more beautiful, he couldn't resist bending over and kissing her on the lips. And so the enchantment was broken and she awakened.

"How long you have been," she said, and smiled up at him.

And suddenly everywhere was life and noise and confusion. The king and queen woke hungry from their deep sleep, and called for their dinner. The cook caught the kitchen boy by the ear and advised him to keep his fingers to himself, or he'd be sorry. The butler, still yawning, bent to mop up the wine that quickly overflowed the jug, and the maid stirred the soup and hurried to serve their majesties.

The horses in the stable and the dogs in the courtyard set up a racket, for they too were more than ready to be fed. The doves cooed contentedly and stirred themselves and flies buzzed in every corner of the castle.

Then the Sleeping Beauty and her prince came down from their tower to announce their wish to be married. The wedding was arranged within the week. After a hundred years asleep everyone was highly excited at the prospect of a royal wedding. It was, after all, exactly what they had been waiting for.

HANSEL AND GRETEL

Once upon a time, on the edge of a deep wood, there lived a poor woodcutter. He had a wife and two children—a boy called Hansel and a girl called Gretel. The wife wasn't the children's real mother, who had died when they were still young. No, the man had married a second time and he often had cause to regret it.

Being poor, the family usually had little to eat, but when there came a hard winter they had even less.

One night the man lay awake in bed, too worried to sleep.

"Oh, wife," he said, "what's going to become of us? We haven't enough food to last the week. Then what will we do?"

"I know exactly what we'll do. We'll take the children into the woods and leave them there. If we're lucky they won't find their way back. Then at least *we* may survive."

"I couldn't think of it," said the man. "Even if they didn't starve to death, wild animals would get them."

"Then we'll all starve," said his wife. "Take your pick, it's either them or us."

The man hated his wife's idea, but he couldn't come up with a better one. Finally she talked him round, which was a way she had, and the man went to sleep with a heavy heart.

But the children were also lying awake. They'd overheard their parents, and now Gretel lay beside her brother crying.

"Oh, Hansel, what are we going to do?" she sobbed.

"Don't cry, Gretel. I won't let anything happen to you."

Hansel got out of bed, put on his clothes and crept outside. The moon was full and shone down, picking out hundreds of white pebbles that glittered like new coins. Hansel collected as many as he could fit into his pockets. Then he crept back to bed.

Early next morning their stepmother woke them roughly.

"Get up, you slugabeds. We're going into the woods. Dress yourselves quickly. Your father and I can't wait all day."

Before they set off she gave them each a crust of bread.

"This is all you'll be getting today, you'd better make it last."

Hansel gave his piece to Gretel, to carry in her apron. His own pockets were full of stones. As they walked along the path into the woods, Hansel kept stopping and turning back.

"Look lively, son," said his father, "you're facing the wrong way."

But Hansel said, "I was just watching the cat, Father. It's sitting on the roof, waving to me."

"Don't be an idiot," snapped his stepmother. "That's not a cat, it's simply the sun shining on the chimney."

But Hansel wasn't really looking back to see the cat. He was stopping, from time to time, to drop a pebble on the path.

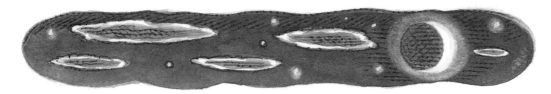

When they were deep into the woods their parents sent the children to collect firewood. Then their father made them a good fire.

"Now, you two sit there and don't wander off," said their stepmother. "Later you can eat your bread and have a rest. We're going to do our work. We shan't be far away. We'll come back for you before it gets dark."

So the children did as they were told and rested and ate their food. They saw no reason to worry, because quite close by they could hear the sound of an axe on wood. Or they thought they could. But it was really a loose branch their parents had carefully tied to a tree so that it knocked against it in the wind. That's what they could hear.

At last, from hunger and boredom, the children fell asleep. When they woke it was getting dark and Gretel was afraid.

"How will we ever find our way home?" she said.

"Don't worry," said Hansel. "Wait till the moon comes up, then we'll have no trouble." Sure enough, when the moon shone down on the pebbles, they stood out clearly, marking a trail that led them all the way home.

It was nearly dawn by the time they reached their house. The children knocked on the door to be let in. When their stepmother saw them standing there, she was furious.

"Fancy staying out all night, you scoundrels. Worrying your father and me like that! We thought you were never coming home."

But now their father could stop worrying. He felt as if a stone had been lifted from his heart. And, for a while, life was kind to them all and they survived.

However, it's usually true that "once poor, always poor". Before long the family was again close to starvation.

"Well, that's the last loaf. When that's gone the crying'll really start," said the man's wife. "This time we must take those children so deep into the woods they'll never find their way out."

Their father had been dreading this. He thought they should all stick together—even if they had to starve. But he'd given in to his wife once and the second time was no different. The man was a coward, and cowards can be cruel too.

Again the children had lain awake and overheard what was said. When their parents were asleep, Hansel got up and tried to go out. But this time his stepmother had locked and bolted the door and he had to creep back into bed. Again he comforted his little sister.

"Don't worry, Gretel. Everything'll be all right. I'll look after you."

The next morning, before the sun rose, their stepmother got them out of bed. She gave them each a small piece of bread and soon they

set off along the path, Hansel, as last time, lagging behind.

"Shake a leg, lad," said his father. "You'll meet yourself coming back, if you're not careful."

"I was just watching the dove, father. It's sitting on the roof, waving to me."

"Fool," said his stepmother. "That's not a dove, it's simply the sun shining on the chimney."

But Hansel wasn't really looking back at the dove. He was stopping, from time to time, to crumble the bread in his pocket and scatter the crumbs along the path.

This time, their parents took Hansel and Gretel far deeper into the woods than last time, further than they'd ever been before. Again their father built a fire and told them to rest and wait until evening when he would come back for them.

At noon the children ate their food. They shared Gretel's piece of bread, because Hansel had crumbled his on the path. Again they fell asleep and only woke when it was already dark. Gretel was afraid, but Hansel assured her that once the moon was up they'd soon find their way home.

However, when the moon rose, there wasn't a single crumb to be seen. Birds had flown down and eaten every one the moment it was dropped. This time there was no trail to follow.

"Don't worry, Gretel," said Hansel. "We'll find our way."

But they didn't. The children walked and walked, through the night and all the next day, hoping they would come to a place they recognised, but they only wandered even deeper into the woods. Tall trees packed tightly together cut out most of the sunshine, and the children walked all day in their shade. They felt cold and helpless. All they could find to eat were a few nuts and berries. At last they were so tired that they fell asleep huddled together beneath a bush.

On the third morning they were still lost, and began to think they might starve to death in that dreadful place.

Suddenly their attention was drawn towards a pure white bird, which perched in the branches above them singing sweetly. When it flew off they began to follow it. The bird came to rest on the roof of a house, in the middle of a clearing. And what a strange house this was.

From a distance it *looked* good enough to eat. When they came closer they found it *was*. The house was made entirely out of gingerbread and cake, and the windows were made of barley sugar. Hansel reached up and took a piece off the roof, and Gretel licked the window pane. The children fell on the house greedily.

Suddenly a voice came from inside.

"*Nibble, nibble, little mouse,*
Who's that nibbling at my house?"

The children didn't stop eating for a moment. They called back,

"*It's only two birds having a rest,*
Borrowing crumbs to build their nest."

Soon both children were gobbling the wall, breaking off huge chunks of cake. They were holding a piece in each hand when the door of the house opened and out came the ugliest old woman you ever saw. Hansel and Gretel were so scared they dropped what they were eating and stood like a pair of statues.

But, to their surprise, the old woman spoke kindly to them.

"Why, what sweet little children! Wherever did you come from? Don't be afraid; come inside and sit down. No one's going to eat you."

And she took them by the hand and drew them into the house. She fed them up with pancakes and honey and milk and baked apples until they couldn't eat another bite. And then she led them upstairs and tucked them into two soft little beds with pure white quilts. The children lay there and thought they must be in heaven.

But they were not—far from it. They were in the hands of a wicked witch who was always in wait for any children who might come her way. She'd made this gingerbread house specially to tempt them in. Once she'd got them inside, she would fatten them up and eat them. Children were her favourite delicacy.

As soon as Hansel and Gretel had come nearby she had smelled them. Witches have a powerful sense of smell, just like animals. This is to make up for their eyes, which are often red, and almost useless. They can hardly see at all.

So the next morning when the witch crept up the stairs on her hard little feet, she had to bend right down low over the children. Only then could she see their round red cheeks. Mmmmm, they made her mouth water.

"These'll make a tasty meal," she said to herself.

She grabbed Hansel with her horrible horny hand, dragged him out of bed and pulled him down the stairs. She took him outside and locked him in a wooden cage. It made no difference to her how he struggled and screamed; witches have no hearts. Then she went back upstairs and roughly shook Gretel too.

"Get up, you lazy lump. Go and get the water and put it to boil. We must cook something special for your brother to fatten him up. Then, when he's a nice rolypoly pudding, I'm going to eat him."

Gretel burst out crying, such terrible tears, but tears too were wasted on the witch. In the end Gretel was made to do as she was told.

From now on Hansel had the very best of food, while poor Gretel had little more than a crab's claw to chew on. Each day the witch went out to check how Hansel was doing.

"Hansel, put out your finger. I want to see if you're fat enough yet."

But instead Hansel poked out a chicken bone and the witch, who couldn't see further than her nose, thought it was his finger. She couldn't understand how, with so much to eat, the boy seemed to get no fatter. After four weeks her patience ran out. She wouldn't wait any longer.

"Well, ready or not, tomorrow we shall chop him up and boil him in a stew."

Then poor Gretel cried. She sobbed and pleaded. She prayed for help. But the witch told her to save her breath.

"Stop your bawling, child, it'll do you no good."

The next day, when Gretel got up, she was ordered to fill the cauldron and hang it over the fire to get the water ready.

"But first we'll do some baking," said the witch. "I've made the dough. You, dear child, can help me by testing the oven. Creep in, there's a good girl, and check it's hot enough."

And she pushed Gretel towards the oven door. Great flames were already pouring out of it. Gretel was no fool; she knew what the witch intended. She would push Gretel inside and bake her; then she would eat her too.

So Gretel said, "I don't know how to tell. And I don't think I could fit in there."

"You stupid child," snapped the witch, pushing Gretel aside. "Have you no brains? Even I could fit in. Look, like this."

And the witch stuck her own head inside the oven door. Then Gretel came up behind her. With an almighty push, she tumbled the witch inside. She slammed the iron door shut and fastened the bolt.

Oh! You should have heard that witch howl! But Gretel didn't wait to listen. She ran off and left her to be baked to a crisp. She ran straight out to Hansel and unlocked his cage.

"Hansel, we're free," she cried out. "The old witch is dead."

Hansel sprang out of the cage and the two of them hugged each other and danced around the yard. The witch was gone, and now they had nothing to be afraid of. The two children went back into the house, and were amazed to find trunks full of pearls and jewels.

Hansel filled his pockets with them. "These are more useful than pebbles," he said. And Gretel too filled her apron until it was overflowing.

"Now, we need to get out of these dreadful woods and find our way home," said Hansel.

They walked for several hours until they came to a lake which stretched before them, blocking their way.

"How can we possibly get across?" said Hansel. "There isn't a bridge or a boat."

"Look," said Gretel. "Over there's a white swan." And she called out and asked the swan to carry them across the water.

The swan came closer and Hansel climbed on her back. "Come on, Gretel," he said.

But Gretel refused, thinking it would be too much for the swan. "Let her take us one at a time," she said.

So that's what the swan did. Once they were both safely across they went on, hoping that they would find their way home. Gradually they came to places they recognised and at last they spotted the chimney of their father's house.

Then, tired as they were, they began to run. They burst through the door and threw themselves upon their father's neck. The poor man thought he must be dreaming, or gone mad. Since he had left his children in the woods, he hadn't known a moment's peace. His wife had left him. She'd been unable to bear his misery at the loss of his children, so that had been some compensation. But all he wanted now was to have his children back.

Gretel emptied her apron of jewels into her father's lap until they spilled on to the kitchen floor and Hansel added his too. Now they need never be poor again. Their worries were at an end, and the three of them could live together in peace and happiness at last.

PUSS IN BOOTS

There was once a poor miller who died leaving to his three sons everything he had in the world: a mill, a mule and a cat. The eldest son took the mill, the second son took the mule and the youngest son, as is often the way in fairy tales, was left with the cat. And he wasn't very pleased with it, I can tell you.

"It's all very well for my brothers, they can at least make a living, but what use is a cat? Even if I skin it and eat it I shall soon be hungry again," he grumbled.

Then the cat spoke up. "Skin me? Don't think off it, master. If you'll get me a bag and a pair of boots, you'll be surprised what I can do for you."

The young man wasn't very hopeful, but he did as the cat asked. After all, he thought, a cat that can talk can't be such a bad bargain.

When Puss had pulled on his smart new boots and thrown his bag over his shoulder, he went off to a nearby rabbit warren. He filled the bag with bran and thistles. Then, leaving the neck wide open, he laid himself down, as if dead, beside it, and waited. He didn't have to wait long before a young and foolish rabbit ventured inside. Quick as a flash, the cat pulled the drawstring tight and that, alas, was the end of the plump little rabbit.

Puss set off immediately for the palace and asked to see the king.

He spoke most politely. "Your Majesty," he said, "please accept this fine young rabbit. It is a gift from my master, the Marquis of Carabas." And he bowed low.

"You may thank your master," said the king, "and tell him how pleased I am with his gift."

Soon after that, the cat hid himself in a cornfield. Again he opened the bag wide and waited patiently until a fat pair of pheasants wandered into it. He drew the string tight and took the birds straight to the king, telling him they were another gift from his master, the Marquis of Carabas. The king was again pleased, and rewarded the cat well.

This went on for two months until Puss became quite a favourite at court.

One day he overheard that the king and his daughter, a most beautiful princess, would be passing by the river on their journey around the kingdom.

"Now is our chance, master," said Puss. "Do as I tell you and your fortune is made. Go down and bathe in the river and leave everything else to me."

The poor young man couldn't begin to see the purpose of this, but he had no other fortune in prospect, so he did as he was told.

While he was bathing, the king's coach passed by and the cat began to cry out in a very loud voice. "Help! Help! My master, the Marquis of Carabas, is drowning."

When the king looked out and saw the cat, whom he recognised, he sent his servants quickly to rescue the Marquis. As they pulled the surprised young man out of the water, the cat approached the king and said, "Your Majesty, my master would like to thank you himself, but while he was bathing some robbers came by and stole all his clothes. He is, of course, far too modest to appear before you without them."

The truth was that the cunning cat had already hidden the clothes carefully beneath a stone, but the king sent off with great haste for a suit of his own to be brought for the Marquis. When he was dressed in it, being a handsome young man, the miller's son looked very presentable. The king clearly approved, and so did the princess. The miller's son gazed back at her fondly too. "We would consider it a pleasure," said the king, "if the Marquis would join us on our tour."

The "Marquis" quickly accepted the invitation and stepped inside the coach.

Puss, as you can imagine, was feeling well pleased with the way his plan was progressing, and he set off swiftly ahead of the coach to prepare the next stage.

He soon came upon some men at work, mowing a meadow, and he said to them in a fierce voice, "Listen to me, my good men. When the king passes by and asks to whom this meadow belongs, be sure to tell him—your master, the Marquis of Carabas—or you'll all be chopped up for cat meat!"

Sure enough, when the king passed by, he asked, "To whom does this meadow belong?"

And the poor, terrified men answered together, "To our master, the Marquis of Carabas." *They* didn't want to be chopped up for cat meat.

The king was impressed, so was the Marquis; it was all news to him.

Next the cat came upon some men reaping corn. Again he said in a fierce voice, "Listen to me, my good men. When the king passes by and asks to whom this cornfield belongs, be sure to tell him—your master, the Marquis of Carabas—or you'll all be chopped up for cat meat!"

The king, passing by soon after, asked, "To whom does this cornfield belong?"

And the reapers answered together, "To our master, the Marquis of Carabas." *They* didn't want to be chopped up for cat meat either.

The king smiled and congratulated the Marquis, and the Marquis smiled back. It was a fine cornfield; he was proud of it.

The cat, who continued ahead of the coach, stopped everyone he met and told them the same thing, until the king was amazed at the vast estates the Marquis owned. There was only one person more

amazed, and that was the Marquis himself. But he kept on smiling and graciously accepting the king's compliments.

Puss came at last to a huge castle. It was the home of a terrible ogre and it was to him that all these lands actually belonged. The cat had taken trouble to learn a little about the ogre and his remarkable powers. He strode up to the castle and asked to be admitted, saying he could not pass by without paying his respects to such an important person.

The ogre received him and invited him to sit down.

"I have heard far and wide of your extraordinary powers," said the cat. "I wanted to see for myself if this could possibly be true. Surely you cannot really turn yourself into any animal you choose; a lion or an elephant, for example."

"Never doubt it," said the ogre. He gave a tremendous roar and turned into a ferocious lion.

This so terrified the cat that he shot out of the window and on to the roof, and didn't venture down again until the ogre turned himself back.

"That was a wonderful feat," said the cat, "but not as wonderful as if you were able to turn yourself into the *tiniest* creature. Now that surely would be impossible?"

"Impossible!" bellowed the ogre. "Impossible . . . "

Instantly he turned himself into a tiny mouse and scuttled across the floor. Then the clever cat did exactly what any cat would have done in his place: he pounced on it and ate it up. One mouthful and it was gone.

Mmm, mmmmm. Puss was still licking his lips when he heard the sound of coach wheels outside. The king, passing by, had noticed the castle and decided to visit. The cat raced downstairs to meet him. He bowed very low.

"Your Majesty is most welcome to the home of my master, the Marquis of Carabas."

"Marquis," said the king, "you certainly kept this secret well."

The Marquis smiled and shrugged his shoulders. It hadn't been difficult. He was just as surprised as the king.

Puss led the king inside. The Marquis escorted the princess, and many loving looks passed between them. In the great hall there was a wonderful banquet prepared, which the ogre had arranged for several of his friends.

After the meal, the king felt very contented. He now had some idea of the great wealth of the Marquis, and he could hardly have failed to notice the whispered words between his daughter and the young man. He decided it was time to drop a hint.

"We have long wished to be able to thank the Marquis for his many gifts. If there is anything we can grant him, he has only to ask."

Then the Marquis, who didn't always need the cat to tell him what to do, bowed and said, "Sire, may I marry your daughter?"

And, since the princess also approved, the wedding took place that very day.

All of them lived happily ever after, including the cat, who became a great lord. He had no need now to be chasing mice, but the truth is that from time to time he still did. But then, a cat is only a cat, after all.

BEAUTY AND THE BEAST

There was once a man who set out on a journey full of hope, but returned in complete despair. Only a year earlier this man had been a rich and respected merchant in the city, but unexpectedly he had lost everything and been forced to move with his family to a small cottage in the country, and there life was hard.

But now word had arrived that a ship had landed carrying valuable cargo that belonged to him, and his family had high hopes of soon returning to their old life. The man said goodbye to his three sons and three daughters, taking with him lists of presents they had begged him to bring back. All except his youngest daughter, Beauty. She was so called because of her lovely face and her sweet nature.

"And what would you like, Beauty?" he asked his favourite child.

"Only your safe return, Father," she said. But when Beauty saw the scornful looks her two sisters gave her, she added, "Perhaps you could bring me a rose. There are so few grow in these parts."

And the man set off, never realising how dear that present would cost him.

When he finally reached the port the man found that the whole cargo had already been sold and used to pay off old debts; there wasn't a penny left. He turned homewards, weighed down with the disappointment he knew his children would feel, and this made his journey seem longer.

He was still thirty miles from home when he lost his way in a forest. A storm blew up, so severe that it more than once threatened to throw him off his horse. He began to search for shelter. He feared that by morning he'd either be frozen to death or eaten by wolves. He could hear them howling close by.

The man saw a light flickering through the trees, and following it he came at last to a very grand house. Normally he would never have dared to approach such a place. But his horse, of its own accord, went into the stables and began to eat hay and oats from a manger. The man headed towards the house.

Although he knocked several times no one came to answer, so the man pushed open the door and entered the hall. There he found a good fire and a table set with silver and crystal and laid with food for one person. He stood before the fire to dry out his clothes, expecting the owner or a servant to appear, but no one came. The house remained silent, apparently deserted.

By eleven o'clock the man couldn't control his hunger and, in desperation, sat down and ate the meal that was waiting there. When he'd finished he set out to discover whose house it was. He passed through many beautiful rooms, high-ceilinged and richly furnished, but he met no one and found no sign of life.

Eventually he came to a small bedroom. The bed was ready-made and warmed, as if a visitor was expected. The man was so tired that he lay down between the soft white sheets and fell asleep. It was past ten in the morning when he woke, completely rested. His adventure the night before now seemed nothing more than a bad dream. Beside his bed he found a set of new clothes and as he dressed the man wondered what kind of spirit it was that was looking after him so well.

When he looked out of his bedroom window the man was surprised to see no evidence of last night's storm, only a perfectly tranquil garden. He went back to the hall and found breakfast waiting for him. He sat down and ate. When he had finished he said out loud, "I'm truly grateful for the hospitality you've shown me, but now I think it's time for me to leave."

Even then no one came near, so the man went in search of his horse. His way to the stables led him through a rose garden and the man suddenly remembered his daughter's request. Sadly he realised that this would be the only present he would manage to take back. He chose the loveliest rose and broke off a single stem.

Instantly there was a terrifying howl. Coming towards him the man saw a dreadful figure, a beast, so hideously ugly that it was almost enough to make him faint.

"You ungrateful wretch! How dare you?" roared the Beast. "After I have saved your life, this is the thanks you show me, to steal the thing I prize above all else. Well, you will die for this."

The man was almost paralysed by fear but he fell on his knees and begged the Beast's forgiveness.

"My lord, do not be angry with me. A flower seemed such a trifle, compared with what you have already done for me. I would never have taken it for myself; it was to fulfil a promise I made to one of my daughters."

"I am no lord, my name is Beast," he snarled. "Don't waste your flattery on me, I despise compliments. Neither am I interested in your excuses. However, since you say you have daughters, I will spare you—if one of them is willing to suffer in your place."

This was no comfort to the man.

"How could I persuade a child whom I love to die for me?" he asked.

"I never spoke of persuasion," said the Beast. "She must come willingly, or not at all. You are now free to leave, but within three months either you or one of your daughters must return. Give me your word on it."

The man offered no argument; he gave the Beast his word. There was no question of sending one of his daughters in his place but at least this way he would be allowed to say goodbye to them all before he died.

"You will not return home penniless," said the Beast. "In your room is a chest. Fill it with whatever you like and I will send it on to you. But do not think to break your promise," he warned. Then the Beast was gone; the man was alone once more.

"Well," he thought, "I must be grateful that my family won't be left poor when I die." He filled the chest with gold pieces, locked it, and went on his way in the deepest despair.

His horse seemed to find its own route and, sooner than he expected, the man reached home, where his family was anxiously waiting for him. Despite their disappointment to see him empty-handed, they were relieved to have him home safe.

When he gave Beauty the rose he'd brought her, the man burst into tears.

"If you had only known how much this rose would cost me, Beauty," he said. And when they'd heard his story Beauty's sisters wept too. They turned on her angrily.

"You're to blame for this. Always trying to be better than us! Now our father will die and all because of you. Yet you stand there calmly, as if you didn't care."

"Why shouldn't I be calm?" asked Beauty. "There's no need for our father to die, because I intend to go in his place. I'd never let him suffer on my account."

Then there was much argument between them.

"No, Beauty, we'll go instead," insisted her brothers. "We'll fight the Beast or die in the attempt."

"There's no point," said their father. "The Beast's far too powerful for us. Anyway, I gave him my word. No, I'm the one to go. After all, my life's nearly over."

But Beauty said, "Father, I won't let you die. My mind's made up. Don't try to persuade me. I shall only follow you." And she persisted until she had convinced them. Her jealous sisters needed no convincing. They were delighted at the thought of getting rid of her. They couldn't have planned it better themselves.

When the man went to bed that night he was surprised to find the chest full of gold in his bedroom. He told Beauty his secret because he trusted her, but decided not to tell his other children. He knew that they would want to return to the city, and he'd made up his mind to stay in the country from now on. However, Beauty persuaded her father to share the gold. While the old man had been away her sisters had been courted by two gentlemen, and the gold would allow them to make good marriages.

But it seemed as if the more love and kindness she showed her sisters the more they resented her. When the time came for Beauty's father to take her to the Beast, the only way the heartless pair could show any sadness at losing her was by rubbing their eyes with an onion.

All too soon Beauty and her father reached the Beast's house. Again the horse made its own way into the stable. When they entered the hall a meal was waiting for them, and despite her own fear Beauty coaxed her father to eat a little.

Without warning, a dreadful noise started up, a kind of deep growling, and there was the Beast beside them. Beauty's father began to tremble and, when she saw the Beast for the first time, so did Beauty; he was even uglier than she'd expected. But when he spoke to her in his terrifying voice, she answered as bravely as she could.

"Well, Beauty, have you come willingly?" he asked.

"Yes," she whispered.

"Good," said the Beast. "I'm glad to see you have kept your

word, old man. In the morning you must leave and never think to return. Goodbye, for now, Beauty." And the Beast went as suddenly as he had come. He left Beauty and her father in a state of terror.

"Oh, my dear, how could I even think of letting you stay here?" said her father. "You must go home and I will remain."

But Beauty was feeling calmer by now. "Don't worry, Father, I'm not afraid. I shall trust fate to take care of me. Let's make good use of the time we have left together. Tomorrow will come soon enough."

At bedtime neither of them expected to rest easily, but the moment their heads touched their pillows they were asleep. Beauty dreamed about a fine lady who said to her, "You have shown great courage in sacrificing yourself for your father. Don't be afraid, your goodness will not go unrewarded."

In the morning Beauty told her father about her dream. It gave them each some comfort, but when it came time for them to part her father wept bitterly.

After he'd left, Beauty wept too, but at length she convinced herself that it served no purpose. If she had only a little time to live then surely she should make the best of it. The house and gardens were very beautiful and she decided to explore them.

She came to a door on which were the words "Beauty's Room". Inside was everything she could have wished for: books without number, musical instruments and plenty of music to play.

She began to think, "If I have only the rest of the day to live, why would such trouble have been taken to please me? Perhaps the Beast doesn't intend to kill me so soon." Feeling more hopeful she picked up a book and opened it. Inside was an inscription:

Welcome, Beauty, do not fear,
You are queen and mistress here.
Whether it be night or day,
Only speak and we'll obey.

"There's nothing else I want," she said aloud, "except to see my poor father, and I know you can't grant that." But even as she spoke she caught sight of the looking glass on the wall. In it she could see moving images: her father arriving home, sad and dejected, her sisters, pretending to be sorry, yet clearly pleased to be rid of her. The next moment the mirror cleared and the picture was gone. But it had given Beauty some comfort and further evidence of the Beast's kindness towards her.

There was food set out for her at midday. While she ate, music played, although she saw no sign of human life. But in the evening, as she was dining, the Beast appeared; the same dreadful noises warned of his approach.

"Beauty, may I sit beside you while you eat?" he asked.

Beauty hardly dared to answer. "You are master here."

"Oh, no," said the Beast, "you are mistress now. I will try to do whatever you wish. But tell me the truth, do you find me hideously ugly?"

Although Beauty hesitated she couldn't bring herself to lie. "You may be ugly, but you've been kind to me and I'm grateful for that."

"Oh, I can be kind," said the Beast, "yet I am still ugly and stupid and unworthy of you. Am I not completely repulsive?"

"No, you're not," said Beauty honestly. "Many people who look handsome have an ugly soul or a cruel heart. It's more important what a person is inside than what he appears outside."

Encouraged by these words the Beast suddenly surprised her by asking, "Beauty, will you marry me?"

Beauty's heart began to beat fast. She was afraid of refusing the Beast, but she couldn't bear the thought of marrying him.

"No, Beast, I won't," she said bravely.

The Beast roared angrily and leaped to his feet and Beauty thought that even now he might kill her. But he left her and she didn't see him again that day.

During the three months that Beauty remained with the Beast she never saw another human being. At mealtimes food was always waiting for her, and unseen hands provided everything she might need. Every evening the Beast joined her while she ate. Rather than dread his visits, she came to look forward to his company. He had little conversation, but he was thoughtful and what he had to say interested her. But each night before he left he caused her the same pain and fear when he asked, "Beauty, will you marry me?"

Every time he asked she refused him. "It would be dishonest to pretend that I might change my mind. I've come to care for you as a friend, and I wouldn't hurt you, but I can't marry you."

"Then promise never to leave me. I feel as if I would die if we were parted," said the Beast.

Beauty could have made this promise easily, but each day she had looked into the mirror and watched her father becoming weaker with worrying about her.

"I would happily stay with you if only I could see my father. Now that my sisters are married and my brothers have left to join the army he's all alone. I know he misses me and it breaks my heart."

"Then go back to him," said the Beast. "I'll die here without you, but I would rather that than have you suffer."

"I don't want to be the cause of your death," said Beauty. "Let me visit my father for one week and then I'll come back and stay with you for ever."

The Beast gave Beauty a ring. "As soon as you are ready to come home, place this ring beside your bed. Goodbye, Beauty, and remember—without you I shall certainly die." With these words in her mind Beauty went to bed, deeply troubled.

When she woke, Beauty found herself in her old bedroom at

home. She went to look for her father, and for the next two hours they sat talking together, unwilling to be parted. At last Beauty went to dress. Word had been sent to tell her sisters that she was home and they were expected shortly.

In her bedroom she found a chest containing the most elegant dresses and exquisite jewellery. Beauty began to share them out to give to her sisters, but the moment she told her father what she was doing the dresses disappeared.

"I think the Beast may have intended the dresses for you," said her father, and the dresses instantly reappeared.

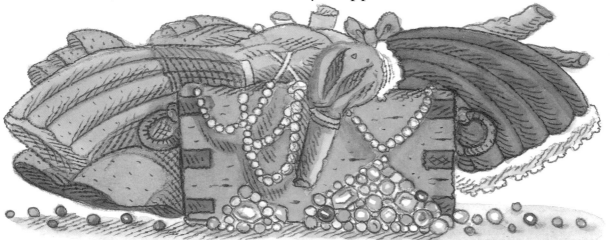

Beauty chose one to wear and hurried to greet her sisters. Having made unhappy marriages, they both looked thoroughly miserable. The eldest had married a handsome but vain man, so full of his own importance that he hardly paid any attention to his wife. The second sister had married a man well-known for his wit and sarcastic tongue, which he used to ridicule everyone around him, especially his wife.

When her sisters saw the wonderful clothes Beauty owned and heard how happy she was living with the Beast, they were bitterly jealous.

"How is it that she always does better than we do?" asked the eldest. "What has she ever done to deserve such good fortune?"

"Nothing," agreed the second sister. "Nothing at all. I could scream. I wish the Beast *had* eaten her. It would have served her right."

The eldest sister smiled at this.

"If we can persuade her to stay longer than a week," she said, "perhaps the Beast will be so angry he really will eat her."

The sisters decided to pretend to be so happy to have Beauty home that she would be unable to leave them for fear of breaking their hearts. They acted their parts so well, showing such love towards her, that Beauty was entirely taken in. When it came time to leave she couldn't bear to upset them and they soon persuaded her to stay. This went on each day until she had been two weeks away from the Beast.

However, Beauty felt wretched at having broken her word and she worried daily how the Beast was managing without her. One night in a dream she saw the Beast lying in his garden, dying of misery. He reproached her, reminding her of her broken promise. Beauty woke up, shivering and crying.

"How could I do such a thing," she asked herself, "when he's treated me with so much kindness? What does it matter if he's ugly? He has a good and generous heart and is far more worthy of love than either of my sister's husbands. I must go back to him. Even if I cannot love him as a husband, I know that I love him as a friend."

She placed the ring beside her bed and went back to sleep. She was greatly relieved when she woke the next morning to find herself back in the Beast's house.

Beauty dressed carefully, wanting to please the Beast. Then she occupied herself as best she could until the time when he was expected to join her. But that time came and passed, and still he didn't appear. Beauty searched first in the house and then the gardens.

She began to feel a dreadful sense of urgency, as if she knew that with each minute that passed her chances of finding him alive were disappearing.

At the point when she felt in complete despair she pictured him as she'd seen him in her dream, and then she knew where to look. Beside the river which flowed along the edge of the garden, she found him lying, almost dead, on a grassy bank.

The sight of him caused her such pain that she dropped to her knees and held him close to her.

"Oh, Beast," she begged, "speak to me. I've treated you so cruelly. Tell me you forgive me."

The Beast stirred and gave a weary sigh. "Is that really you, Beauty? Now I can die in peace."

"Don't think of dying," she said. "I've come back and I'll never leave you again. I thought that I loved you only as a friend, but now I can see that I can't live without you. I want to be your wife."

The words were barely spoken before there were strange, echoing sounds in the air around them, a shimmering quality to the light and at the same time a transformation in the Beast. These strange happenings lasted hardly a minute and when they were over Beauty found herself looking at a young and handsome man, who lay smiling up at her.

He began to explain, but she would hardly let him speak before she felt compelled to ask, "Where is my Beast gone?"

"He's here, before you, trying to tell you how you have saved his life," laughed the young man. "A cruel fairy imprisoned me in the skin of the Beast until a time when a good and beautiful woman agreed to be my wife. You have freed me and now I can ask you in my own right: Beauty, will you marry me?"

Once she was certain that this was the same Beast she had come to love, albeit in a different form, she gladly accepted.

They returned to the house where they found Beauty's family waiting for them and also the fine lady whom Beauty recognised from her dream.

"You have done well," she told Beauty. "Your goodness and generous spirit have brought happiness both to yourself and your prince. Your wisdom will make you a good queen. As for your sisters," she said, turning to face them, "until you truly regret your past wickedness, you will stand outside your sister's palace as a pair of statues. There you will be able to see the rewards she has earned and consider how different your own lives might have been."

Then all of them were transported to the prince's own kingdom where Beauty married the prince and lived happily, just as she deserved.

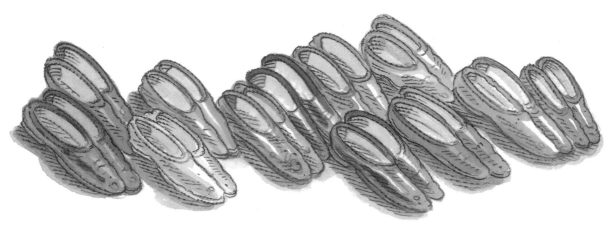

THE TWELVE DANCING PRINCESSES

Long ago, in another time, in another country, there lived a king who had twelve daughters, all equally beautiful and yet entirely different. The king was possessive of his daughters. Each night he locked and bolted the door of the bedroom where they slept in twelve identical beds. But every morning, when he unlocked the door, what should he find waiting for him but twelve pairs of satin slippers worn into holes, as if they'd been danced in the whole night long.

Nobody could discover how this came to happen, nor where the princesses went to dance—and *they* weren't telling anyone. But the king was determined to find out. There was a limit to how many new pairs of slippers he was prepared to buy.

He announced throughout the kingdom that anyone who could solve the mystery of the slippers could choose which of the princesses he wanted to marry. In time the young man would also inherit the throne. But if, after three days and nights, anyone who tried should fail, then . . . he would pay for it with his life.

Now you might have thought that this would put off even the most determined suitor. Not at all. Stories of the twelve beautiful princesses spread far and wide. There was no shortage of young men waiting to take up the challenge.

The first, a king's son, arrived at the palace, was introduced to the twelve princesses, and immediately fell in love with every one of them. After supper he was taken to a small room next to the princesses' bedchamber. That night, so that he could keep his eye on them, the door to their bedroom was left open.

The young prince struggled to stay awake, but no matter how hard he tried, sleep soon got the better of him. The next thing he knew it was morning. There, as usual, was the evidence, arranged neatly in a row. And the next night the same; and the third night also. And on the fourth morning he lost his life, just as the king had promised.

Over the months many young men lost their hearts, and then their heads, but the mystery remained. The king was in a permanent rage.

About that time a poor soldier, returning from a war in a distant country, stopped to rest in a wood. He sat beneath a tree, eating the last of his food. An old woman approached him and he offered her half of what he had.

After they'd eaten, the old woman asked the soldier, "Where are you headed now?"

"Wherever my nose leads and my feet follow," he said. "Perhaps to the palace yonder. If I can discover where the twelve princesses dance at night, happen they'll make me king."

The soldier laughed at the idea, but the old woman didn't.

"Happen they will," she said, "as long as you remember not to drink any of the wine the princesses offer you. Just pretend to drink it, then pretend to fall asleep. If you wear this cloak you'll be invisible, so you can follow them and find out where they go."

She handed him a small bundle of cloth. It felt as light and fragile as a spider's web.

The soldier couldn't decide whether to take the old woman seriously. However, he didn't want to hurt her feelings so he thanked her and went on his way. The moment he was out of sight, he unrolled the cloak and threw it over his shoulder. Immediately half of him disappeared. He took it off and there he was whole again. He threw it over his other shoulder and that half disappeared too. In great excitement, the soldier rolled up the cloak, put it in his bundle and set off for the palace.

Despite his poor appearance, he was treated as well as the others. When it came to bedtime, he was taken to the same small room next to the royal bedchamber. Sure enough, in came the eldest princess carrying a glass of wine, but the soldier was prepared for her. He took the glass and pretended to sip the wine, but in fact he let it run down his chin and soak into a sponge he had tied beneath his beard. Then he closed his eyes. In a moment he appeared to be sound asleep.

The eldest princess returned to her sisters, who laughed when they heard the soldier's heavy snoring.

"Poor fool," said the eldest princess. "He'd have done better to have saved his handsome head. Come now, it's time for us to get ready."

The princesses opened their cupboards and drawers and pulled out their finest clothes. The soldier, next door, listened to their footsteps almost running around the room. He heard the excitement in their voices as they dressed themselves and arranged their hair. But one voice sounded less happy than the others. It was the voice of the youngest princess.

"I don't know why," she said, "but I have a terrible feeling that something's going to go wrong."

"Faintheart," said her eldest sister. "Always the worrier. Nothing's going to go wrong. How many times have we done this? How many young men have we outwitted? This one looked so tired he'd have fallen asleep without any help from me."

When they were ready, the princesses peeped around the door. Seeing the soldier fast asleep, they smiled, thinking they were quite safe. Then the eldest princess stood beside her bed and clapped her hands three times. The bed slid aside and a trapdoor appeared, with a staircase leading down into the ground. The princesses went through the trapdoor, in order of age, the eldest leading the way. Last came the youngest princess, still looking unhappy.

The soldier jumped up. Wrapping the cloak around him, he followed close on her heels. So close that at one point he caught the hem of her dress.

"Oh! What was that?" she cried out. "Someone stepped on my dress. I felt it."

"Nonsense," said the eldest. "There's no one there. It probably caught on a nail in the wall. Come along and stop worrying."

They hurried on and the youngest followed, but she kept looking over her shoulder as if she knew someone was following her.

When the princesses reached the bottom of the staircase, they passed along a corridor which led to a low door. They bobbed their heads and stepped out into a small wood. Here, even though there was no moon, it was perfectly light, because the leaves of all the trees were made of silver and shone in the dark. Next they came to a wood where the leaves of all the trees were gold, and glowed softly. Finally they came to a third wood where the leaves were diamonds, which sparkled and spangled the air like a thousand stars.

The soldier was quite certain that no one would believe this, so he broke off a branch of each tree to take back with him. The snapping sounds rang out like shots in the silence. Every time, the youngest princess gasped out loud.

"What was that? There, didn't I tell you something was wrong?"

But the eldest princess said, "It's nothing to worry about. It's only our princes firing a salute to welcome us. Hurry, they must be waiting for us."

At the edge of the third wood was a lake, and on the shore were twelve little boats. In each sat a handsome prince waiting to row across the water.

Each of the princesses stepped into a boat. The soldier climbed in after the youngest princess. Their boat rocked for a moment, but then settled low in the water. The prince who rowed this boat soon began to get tired.

"How is it," he wondered aloud, "that we are moving so much more slowly than the others, even though I'm working just as hard at the oars?"

The youngest princess stared at the part of the boat which sat so low in the water and the soldier stared back at her. Even though it was such a warm evening she couldn't help shivering.

Soon they came in sight of an island on which there was a fabulous castle, alive with lights. From every window poured the sound of music. The princesses hurried as if they couldn't wait to begin dancing. They danced all night with their partners, but never seemed to get tired.

The soldier watched and even joined in, but nobody saw him. Once or twice the youngest princess felt a hand on her waist, or someone brush her dress. Yet, when she looked, no one was there. Whenever she reached for her glass of wine it was already empty.

"Someone keeps drinking my wine," she said, almost in tears.

"You must have drunk it yourself," insisted the eldest princess. "Do stop fussing and try to enjoy yourself." But the youngest princess couldn't do that. Something was wrong and she knew it.

The princesses danced on through the night, until their slippers were all in holes. Only then were they ready to leave. The princes led them to the boats. This time the soldier, tired of teasing the youngest princess, climbed into the boat of the eldest sister.

As the boat moved over the lake the soldier watched her, with the

bright diamond light on her face. Even though the princesses were all beautiful, to him she was the most beautiful.

When the boats reached the other shore, the princesses said goodbye to their princes and promised to meet them again the next night. Then they hurried through the three small woods until they reached the low door. The soldier raced past and up the stairs, before they could discover him missing.

By the time the twelve princesses looked in on him, he was sound asleep, just as they'd left him, snoring fit to wake the dead. They took off their worn-out slippers and left them in a row. They went to bed thinking their secret was as safe as ever.

In the morning the soldier could hardly believe what had happened. So much of it seemed like a dream. He decided that he wouldn't speak to the king until he'd had another chance to test his memory.

That night everything happened exactly as before. The soldier enjoyed himself so much that when it came to the third night he couldn't resist the opportunity to follow them again. This time he took back with him a golden goblet as further proof.

On the fourth morning, when the king summoned the soldier, the twelve princesses hid themselves behind a screen, to hear what he had to say. The king wasn't at all hopeful—he'd been disappointed before—but this time proved different.

When he asked, "Well, have you discovered where my daughters dance each night?" The soldier replied, "With twelve princes in an underground castle."

The king found this difficult to believe, so it was fortunate for the soldier that he had proof. He told the king all about the trapdoor and the staircase leading to the underground wood. Then he took out the three branches from the silver and gold and diamond trees and showed him the golden goblet.

The king called for his daughters and asked each one, beginning with the youngest, if the soldier's story was true. Each princess in turn hung her head and said nothing, she couldn't deny it. But the eldest spoke out and said, "The soldier's right, Father, he's been too clever for us."

"Then you may choose which of them you will marry," the king told the soldier.

The soldier, who wasn't a young man himself, chose the eldest princess, or as he put it, 'the most beautiful'. And this pleased the eldest; she liked a man with brains.

The marriage took place soon after. There were eleven lovely bridesmaids and a splendid feast with music and dancing that went on and on, for days and days. And over the years there were other weddings and other celebrations, and always some excuse for dancing in the palace.

RUMPELSTILTSKIN

Now this story is about a poor miller who never knows when to hold his tongue; it's always getting him into bother. This miller has a daughter, pretty as a picture, and clever—she has brains enough for the pair of them. He's forever boasting about all the things she can do, but one time he goes too far, and this is how it happens.

The miller has some business with the king and when it's done he soon gets round to his favourite subject.

He says to the king, "I have a daughter, Your Majesty, such a beauty she puts the sun to shame."

Now the king's hardly likely to be interested in a miller's daughter; he's already bored.

"And clever," says the miller, "there's nothing my daughter can't do."

The king yawns. The miller's desperate to impress him.

"Why, she can even . . . spin straw into gold," says he.

Spin straw into gold! Now the king's listening; he's all ears. This king loves gold more than anything in the world. He can't get enough of it.

He says to the miller, "I'd like to meet your daughter. Send her to the palace. We'll see if she can really do as you say. But I warn you, if you've lied to me, she'll lose her head."

So the miller goes home and tells his daughter what he's done.

"Oh, father!" says the girl. "That's a fine mess you've got me into. You and your big mouth. Now what'll I do?"

Well, what can she do? When a king says do a thing, you best do it; nobody argues with a king. So the girl puts on her smartest clothes and takes herself off to the palace.

When she gets there the king shows the girl into a large room. There's nothing in it but a stool, a spinning wheel and stacks and stacks of straw.

"Now," says he, "let's see you spin this straw into gold by morning or else it'll be off with your head."

And he locks the door and leaves her there.

The girl may be clever, but she isn't that clever. She doesn't know *what* to do so she stamps her feet and throws her apron over her head. She howls, more out of frustration than fear.

When she finally stops to draw breath she hears a scritch, scratching noise at the window. Up she gets and opens it and in leaps a little wee man. He's got eyes like pieces of coal and dangly

legs and his hands look just itching to pinch something. And all the while he's grinning.

"What's up with you?" says he.

"What's it to you?" says she.

"Don't hurt to tell," says he.

"S'ppose it don't," says she. And she tells him the whole story, first and last, and then she bursts out crying again.

"And it can't be done," says she.

"I can do it," says he. "You watch me."

The girl looks at him, to see if he's serious.

"What'll it cost?" says she, suspicious-like.

"That necklace'll do," says he, reaching out his little grabby hand. So the girl gives it him.

There and then he sits himself down on the stool and he's off. Whirl, whirl, whirl, three times round, and the bobbin's full of shining gold thread. Then whirl, whirl, whirl, and there's another one. As easy as that. No matter how close the girl watches she can't see the trick of it.

In the end she lies down on a small heap of the straw and sleeps while the little wee man does all the work for her. When she wakes he's gone and the room's bright with shining gold.

Come morning, the king unlocks the door and he's highly delighted. He takes one look at the gold and he wants more. He leads the girl to an even bigger room with stacks and stacks and stacks of straw.

"Well, you've done it once," he says, "let's see you do it again. Spin all this straw into gold by morning—if you want to keep that pretty head of yours."

And he locks the door and takes away the key.

She doesn't know what to do. She's been lucky once, but a second time . . . She sits and stares at the straw.

After a time—a long time, a short time, who knows how long she sits staring—the girl hears the same scritch, scratching sound at the window.

Well, up she jumps and lets in that little wee man. He stands there grinning. *He* can see what *she's* thinking, and she can read his mind equally well.

"I've only got this ring left," says she.

"That'll do," says he, plucking it off her finger.

Then down he sits and he's off. Whirl, whirl, whirl, three times round and the bobbin's full. The girl lies down and the sound of the wheel, whirl, whirl, whirl, soon lulls her to sleep.

When she wakes it's as if the sun's come inside the room, it makes her eyes ache to look at it. The king arrives and his eyes fair pop out. He looks at the girl and he thinks, 'She's only a miller's daughter but she's right pretty and she's already made me very rich.'

But the man's greedy, oh he's greedy, all right. This time he leads her to a great barn of a room that's so full of straw she can hardly fit through the door.

"Now, my dear," says he, "if you can spin this straw into gold I'll make you my wife. But if you can't, well . . . "

He doesn't need to spell it out. By now she knows what it'll cost her. The girl sits down totally at a loss. Even suppose the little wee man comes again, he won't help her for nothing—and nothing's all she's got left to give him.

Sure enough she hears his fingers scritch, scratching at the window. She ups and opens it and in he comes, grinning as usual. His bony little shoulders are shaking, he's that pleased with himself.

"Before you ask," says she, "I've nothing else to give you. And that's the truth."

But the little wee man says, "I can still help you—if you'll promise me your firstborn child."

'Child!' thinks the girl. 'I'm not even married yet.'

That's far off in the future, she'll worry about that when and if it happens. For now she has herself to think about.

"All right," says she, "only do hurry up."

There's that much straw this time she's worried he'll not be done by morning. But the little wee man sets to work and spins faster than ever, so fast it makes her dizzy to watch. Whirl, whirl, whirl, like a whirlwind.

When the king comes in next day he looks like the cat that got the cream. He's found himself a real beauty for a wife and now he has more gold than he could have dreamed of.

True to his word, the pair are straightway married. They live happily enough for over a year. They have a bonny little baby that they dote on. The queen's clean forgot the promise she made, and she's forgot all about the little wee man. That's convenient, isn't it?

But promises have a way of coming back to haunt you. When the baby's just old enough to have worked his way into her heart the queen has a visitor, and not a welcome one neither. The little wee man suddenly appears in her room.

"That child's mine," says he. "Hand him over."

But the queen'd die first. She clutches the baby to her. She'd swallow him to keep him safe.

"You're not having him," says she. "I'll give you anything else." She offers him a horse, a house, a palace . . . the entire riches of the kingdom—but that don't work.

"Riches are nothing to me. It's that babby I want. Come on, a promise is a promise."

Then the queen sets up crying. She howls and she sobs, she weeps and she wails, as if her heart'll break. Such a carry-on, and lucky for her it seems to work.

"All right, all right, all right," says the little wee man. He can't a–bear the sound of crying. "I'll tell you what I'll do. I'll give you three days to come up with my name. If you manage it you can keep him. But don't build your hopes," says he. And he stretches out his poky little hand towards the baby. The queen snatches him away.

The little wee man sneers and says, "Guess me in nine or that babby's mine." And off he goes, fair puffed up with conceit.

Well, the poor queen never sleeps that night. She sits up making lists and lists of all the names she can think of. Next morning she sends messengers off, up and down the country, to see what they can find. It won't be any ordinary name, that much she knows.

At dusk when the little wee man appears at the window the queen's ready for him.

"Now," says he, "have you guessed my name?"

"Is it Nehemiah?" says she.

"No, it's not," says he.

"Is it Obadiah?" says she.

"No, it's not," says he.

"Then it must be Zachariah," says she.

"Oh, no, it's not that neither," says he, and he grins fit to split his face. And away he goes triumphant. So that's one chance she's lost.

The second day the queen asks everyone around but the more names she collects the harder it is to choose. She starts to think of all the names she'd *like* to call him.

That night when he comes he says, "All right, what's my name?"

"Is it Hornyhands?" says she.

"No, it's not," says he, although it could have been.

"Is it Skinnyshanks?" says she.

"No, it's not," says he. But that would've suited him too.

"Well, is it Grinningidiot?" says she.

"Oh, no, it's not," says he, grinning even harder.

He looks at her with eyes like burning coals and he says, "Only tomorrow and that babby's mine. Three more'll make nine, then he's mine, mine, mine."

Off he goes, laughing and shrieking. And that's her second chance gone.

Then it's the third day. She's all but given up hope when the last of her messengers returns. He's got no new names for her but he does have a strange story to tell.

As he was making his way home he passed through a wood and in a clearing he spied a weird little man dancing round a fire and singing to himself:

> "*Tonight I brew, tonight I bake,*
> *Tomorrow the Queen's little babby I take.*
> *She can't win this little game,*
> *For Rumpelstiltskin is my name.*"

Well, when she hears this the queen's fit to burst with excitement. She can't wait for the little man to come that night. When she opens the window, in he leaps and ooh, he looks so pleased with himself. His little black eyes are shining and he's wriggling, as if his body won't keep still. The queen pretends to be real scared of him.

"Now, then, my lovely, what's my name?" says he.

"Ermm, is it Abberdabber?" says she.

"No, it's not," says he, and he comes a little closer.

"Oh dear, is it Bobanob?" says she.

"No, it's not," says he, coming even closer and grinning from ear to ear. Then he points his bony finger at her and he says, "Take your time, my beauty. One more guess and that babby's mine."

He's close enough now to reach out and touch the baby. So the queen steps back a little and then she breaks out grinning too.

"Well, could it be Rumpelstiltskin by any chance?"

The little wee man shrieks, "Who told you! Who told you? The devil must have told you."

Then BANG! he stamps so hard his right leg disappears into the floor. Then BANG! he stamps his other leg and that goes down too. Then whoosh! right through the hole and he keeps on going, down, down, down into the ground until he's clean disappeared. All that's left is the hole.

And as sure as five and five make ten, nobody ever saw *him* again. And that's a true story, or my name isn't. . . .

THE PRINCESS AND THE PEA

Once upon a time there was a prince who wanted to marry, so what did he do? He looked for a princess, of course. But she had to be a *real* princess. Nothing else would do. He travelled all over the world to find one, but without success.

There were plenty to choose from, at least, plenty who *said* they were real princesses. But the prince could never be sure.

There were no end of beautiful girls who put the sun to shame. There were any number of girls who could sing as sweetly as a bird and a dozen who could dance and wear out a pair of slippers in an evening. There were countless girls who were immensely rich and even more who had *been* rich, but now were terribly poor. There was no shortage of girls who had ugly sisters and cruel step-mothers. There were one or two girls who told him they'd been locked up in towers, and one who claimed she'd been to sleep for a hundred years! There was even a girl who said she'd once kissed a frog. But no matter what they told him, the prince never knew whether to believe them. He could never be *absolutely* sure.

Finally the prince returned home, sad and disappointed, because he had so set his heart on finding a real princess.

His mother, the queen, hated to see her son so despondent.

"Don't worry, my dear. When the right girl comes along, I shall know how to tell. You leave it entirely to me."

One night there was a terrible storm in the city. The heavens opened and the rain fell in sheets like a waterfall. There was thunder and lightning. Something had upset the weather and now it was taking out its temper on the world.

Suddenly there was a loud knocking at the city gates and the king himself went to see who was there. When he opened the gates he saw a most forlorn and pathetic figure, who said she was a princess.

She was soaked to the skin. Her hair was dripping wet and hung like rats' tails. Her clothes were sticking to her, and even her shoes were awash with water. To be blunt about it, she looked a poor, bedraggled creature, but she *said* she was a real princess.

And that was the truth, she was. She was presently on her travels around the world, in search of a prince. She was now old enough to marry and had set her heart on finding a *real* prince; nothing else would do. She had already met plenty who *said* they were real princes, but somehow she had a feeling they weren't.

There were no end of handsome young men who only had to be looked upon to be loved. There were any number of brave young men who had apparently slain dragons or demons or devils—some said with their bare hands. There were countless young men who had been turned into beasts, or birds, or frogs. There was even one young man who said he had hacked his way through a hedge, half a mile deep, to rescue a princess.

But no matter what they told her, the princess couldn't bring herself to believe them. She could never be *absolutely* sure.

And so here she was, still on her travels, feeling sad and disappointed. She had *so* set her heart on finding a real prince.

When the royal family first saw her, dripping on the palace floors, they were not easily convinced either. How could they tell if she were a real princess, the state she was in? The poor prince was as confused as ever. But the queen knew exactly what to do.

"Come with me," she told him. "We'll soon find out."

They went together to the bedchamber, where the princess was to sleep. The queen told the prince to take the mattress off the bed. Then she laid a single pea on the base of the bed. On top of it, they laid twenty mattresses. And then, on top of those, they laid twenty feather beds. And that was the bed the princess was to sleep in.

All through the night the princess lay awake. She tossed and she turned. She wriggled and she jiggled in the bed to try to make herself more comfortable, but it was no use. By morning she was perfectly miserable.

When she came down to breakfast, the queen asked, "Did you sleep well, my dear?"

But the princess replied, "No, I'm afraid I didn't. In fact, I hardly closed my eyes. I don't know when I've had such a bad night's sleep. There must have been something in the bed, because this morning I am covered in bruises. How I have suffered!"

And then the prince *knew* that she must be a real princess. Who else could have felt a single pea through twenty mattresses and twenty feather beds? Only a real princess would be so sensitive.

"For years, I have been looking for a real princess," said the prince. "Now that I've found you, will you marry me?"

The princess considered this carefully. If he could know with such certainty that she was a *real* princess, which she was, then surely it must follow that he was indeed a *real* prince too. (And he was.)

Now, when a real and handsome prince meets a real and beautiful princess, it's only natural that he should ask her to marry him. And what could be more natural than for her to accept? So she did.

And what should they both do then? Why, live happily ever after, of course. And they did.

And so, I hope, will you.